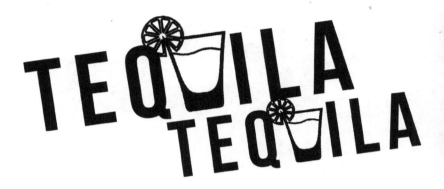

EMMA HART

NEW YORK TIMES BESTSELLING AUTHOR

ONE

ASPEN

Tequila Te-Tap-Tap

IT WAS A UNIVERSALLY ACCEPTED TRUTH that sleeping with your best friend was a very, very bad idea.

Just because it worked out for Chandler Bing and Monica Geller didn't mean it was meant for everyone.

Of course, not that I was thinking of that right now.

Nope.

At this moment, I was pressed against the rock-solid body of my best friend. His fingers were wound in my messy hair, making it even more of a disaster, and mine were scrunching his shirt up.

And yes, we were kissing.

I know. I got nothin'.

It was all the tequila's fault. We'd had too much, and what had started as an attempt for him to help me to bed had ended up with me falling into the doorframe, giggling, and him…

Well, kissing me.

I was fuzzy on how it happened. In fact, given the sheer amount of tequila I'd consumed tonight, I was fuzzy on just about everything.

The one thing I was perfectly clear about was that I was kissing him back. Very enthusiastically.

And, you know, I couldn't even stop it. I wasn't entirely sure how it started, but it was a pretty damn good kiss. A bit sloppy, sure, but then we were both drunk. It wasn't going to be a soul-stealing kiss now, was it?

Let's face it—kissing was kinda messy, even when you were sober, never mind when you were stupid drunk and lacked the most basic coordination.

Luke pulled away from me and looked at me with bright blue eyes. "I'm sorry."

"For what?" I asked.

Look at that. I didn't slur my words. Go drunk Aspen!

"Kissing you." He bit his full bottom lip. "It was an accident."

I snort-giggled, falling forward into him. I smooshed my face into his chest as the giggles took hold of me, making me stagger forward.

"Whoa," he laughed, holding me up even though he was unsteady himself. "Why are you laughing?"

Craning my neck back to meet his eyes, I pressed one finger to my lips. "Shh," I whispered. "Because I can feel that you're not sorry."

He stared at me, blinking so that his thick, dark eyelashes cast little shadows over his pretty little cheeks.

Wow, yeah. I was hammered. Pretty cheeks? Was there such a thing as that?

"What?" Luke didn't move.

Sober Aspen wouldn't say the next words. Sober Aspen was boring. "Your penis is very hard," I whispered, nodding firmly. "And it wants to play."

"What is it? A kitten?" He laughed, taking a step back.

"Noooo! I have the pussy!"

Luke tripped over my hairbrush on the floor and fell back onto my bed. His laughter echoed off the walls, and he almost bounced right off onto the floor.

I sniggered, but before I could get control of my own feet, I slipped on thin air and fell into my dresser. My hip slammed into the corner, and I screamed, "Fuck!"

"What? Are you okay?" Luke stumbled as he stood up.

"No! My dresser is trying to kill me!"

He took hold of me and pulled me to the bed. It was a miracle we didn't fall over again, to be honest. My room was a hot mess and looked like ten teenage girls lived there. We couldn't all be perfect.

"Here. Come here." He lay me back on the bed and

went for my shorts.

I squirmed away. "What are you doing?"

His eyes went wide. "Checking your hip."

"Oh. Okay." I giggled again and rolled onto my side to let him check it. Pain shot through me as my hip touched the bed. "Whoops! Wrong hip!"

"How do you mess that up?"

"Tequila." I rolled to face him and tapped my temple. "Very influential, but a complete asshole. It should be a politician."

"So could you with all the shit you talk when you're drunk." He chuckled and pulled up my shirt, then carefully moved down the waistband of my jeans to check my hip.

I peered down. The skin was grazed, and even drunk me knew there'd be one hell of a bruise there in two days' time. Excellent. That was what I needed at the start of the summer.

A shiner on my hip.

"It doesn't look too bad." Luke's fingers brushed across the tender skin, his rough fingertips making my skin tingle.

"You think?" I tilted my head up to meet his eyes and froze.

His face was right there. The lips I'd been kissing just minutes ago were close enough to mine that one twitch, and they'd be touching mine again.

Maybe I was crazy. Maybe it was the tequila.

No, it was definitely the tequila, and I was definitely crazy, but for the purpose of what I was about to do, it would be easier to use the tequila as an explanation.

I kissed him.

I kissed my best friend square on the lips. *Deliberately.*

I thought he'd pull away, but he didn't. His gentle touch on my hip became a hard grip as he yanked my body into his. He was most definitely still hard, and I was damn glad we'd had enough tequila that this would be forgotten in the morning.

Because if there was anything you wanted to forget, it was making out with your best friend.

And him touching your boob.

Which he was doing right now.

Oh, sweet Jesus. This was happening.

I decided to stop thinking. Thinking wasn't going to change this, and hell, it was my fault. I'd kissed him again.

I fell into the kiss. And him, literally. The next few minutes was a mess of awkward touching and kissing and getting more turned on than I had any right to be by my best friend.

Before my drunken brain could compute it, we were both removing our clothes, stripping ourselves down to be totally naked. Then we were kissing again, our teeth almost clashing as I slipped when we came together. Giggles were drowned out by moans as Luke slipped his hand between my legs and worked my clit with his fingers.

I reached toward him and took his hard cock in my hand. His teeth grazed my lips, and when his hips bucked, he pulled away from me and met my eyes.

"Condom?"

I pointed in the general direction of my nightstand.

What?

Just because I hadn't been laid in six months didn't mean I wasn't optimistic it could happen at any time.

I giggled at that thought. Who'd have guessed it'd be my best friend who'd end my sexual drought?

Luke staggered as he got to his feet. I hiccupped, clapping my hands over my mouth when he laughed and rummaged through my top drawer. Coming up empty, he moved to the second draw, and my eyes widened as he plucked my little purple bullet vibrator out and held it out with a questioning eyebrow.

Inside, Sober Aspen was dying of embarrassment.

Drunk Aspen laughed her ass off.

Sober Aspen was going to hate Drunk Aspen in around twelve hours.

He dropped it back into the drawer and plucked out a box of condoms. Like I said; I was forever optimistic that a deity would drop a porn star or someone equally as talented on my doorstep for a quickie.

Another giggle erupted from me when I watched Luke fumble with the condom. He almost dropped it before he finally managed to roll it on himself. It was like watching a cat try to open a door or hold onto something.

"Shut up," he muttered, holding the condom in place as he came back to me.

I laughed, lying back. He slipped easily between my legs, and he kissed me several times before he tried to push inside me.

I jerked back up the bed like his cock was on fire. "Luke, that's my ass."

He stopped, stepped back, and bent down. "Whoops."

"Whoops? You nearly impaled my ass and you say *whoops?*"

"Shh." He touched a finger to my lips and tried again.

Thankfully, this time, he got it right.

His pushed his cock inside my pussy slowly, leaning forward to kiss me again. I gripped his shoulders as he started to move. Within three thrusts his cock fell out, but he slipped it back inside me—after a second, that was.

I wrapped my legs around his waist so it didn't happen again. We kissed hard, and I tilted my hips so he could thrust deeper.

It was a mistake.

He groaned.

And I knew.

I just *knew* what was going to happen. He was going to come, and I wasn't even close. Not even warmed up. The key was in the car, but the engine wasn't revving. No sir, not even close to it.

So, I did the only thing a self-respecting twenty-four-year-old woman not about to orgasm could do.

I faked it.

Moan. Clench. Grab. Moan. Arch. Writhe.

And moan again.

Just as I suspected, Luke came.

And it was goddamn miserable.

Tap tap squirt, indeed.

He collapsed on top of me for a minute, and I faked that post-orgasmic haze of heavy breathing and random twitches of muscle.

Luke pulled out of me and rolled away, reaching immediately for the condom. I took my chance and got up, pretending to be on shaky legs until I left the room.

Then I ran to the bathroom and locked myself in there.

Dear God, what had I done? Thank God two minutes of bad sex didn't make me sober. Nobody needed to be sober after that.

I peed, washed my face, and grabbed this morning's tank top from the floor. It proclaimed me to be a people hater—accurate—and I made my way back to my room, using the door to help me stay upright.

Apparently, the tequila was getting its second wind.

Pausing outside the door, Sober Aspen broke through just long enough to convince Drunk Aspen to go into the kitchen and take some aspirin and drink some water.

Drunk Aspen was smart. She listened.

Aspirin and water down my throat, I finally reached my destination: my bed.

And someone was looking down on this idiot because Luke was already fast asleep. Thankfully, he wasn't on my favorite side of the bed, so I didn't have to attempt to shift his naked ass over.

Let's be honest. I'd probably break my ankle trying to do it after this much alcohol.

I pulled some clean panties from the dresser and almost fell over trying to put them on, so I aborted that idea and, instead, stumbled my way over to my side of the bed and sat down to put them on.

Mission accomplished with my poor vagina tucked away inside my panties, I tucked myself into bed and rolled over, putting my back to my very naked best friend.

Sleep came for me in seconds, and I'd never been gladder.

TWO

ASPEN

Pancakes and Other Necessary Bullshit

I CREPT OUT OF MY BED WHILE LUKE WAS STILL asleep. He'd rolled over at some point in the night and was now lying on his stomach with his bare ass in the air.

If I didn't feel like the walking dead, I'd have taken a minute to admire how white his ass was compared to the rest of his tanned body. Being part Mexican, he had an unfair advantage on the rest of us already when it came to a tan.

Like I would admit part of my tan came from a bottle.

I grabbed some bright pink shorts from the top of my laundry basket and gave them a sniff. They didn't smell like they'd been worn—and there was a good chance they hadn't been—so I pulled them on and quietly made my way into the kitchen.

More aspirin and water were my first stop, and my second was to sink onto one of the stools at the little island in the middle of my kitchen and groan.

Unfortunately, my night's sleep hadn't had the effect I thought it would.

Namely, I could still remember the disaster that was last night. The two whole minutes of the worst sex of my life with one of the most important people in it.

What a disaster. This is why you're warned about excessive drinking, kids. Not because of liver failure. Because you might just fuck yourself up by sleeping with your best friend.

I sighed and ran my fingers through my hair until they reached my bun, looking out of my window. I could see nothing but trees since my apartment block backed onto the park. It beat hearing kids scream every time I opened my windows—not that I did that a lot in Texas.

That would be insane.

What was I supposed to do now? I knew Luke well enough to know that he'd come out of my room with questions about why he was naked.

What the hell did I say?

Oh, yeah, we had sex, and it was fucking dreadful.

No. I couldn't do that. I couldn't even say we had sex. If he mentioned it, then sure, but I couldn't bring it up. No way.

Let's be honest. The sex was exponentially better for him than it had been for me.

I'd faked more than a few orgasms in my life, but I never imagined I'd be faking one with my best friend.

Then again, I never imagined I'd be banging him either.

I sat up and covered my mouth with my hands. This had the potential to ruin our friendship. Good sex may not have been an issue, but bad sex? The worst sex ever?

Yep. That meant it was a goner.

Nope. My only option was to sit here and hope like hell he didn't remember it. He'd been as drunk as I had, and the only reason I remembered was because I had an unfortunately good memory and drank water before I went to sleep.

He hadn't done that. He'd pumped and dumped and passed out.

I needed to be normal. I couldn't be sitting here like a loser when he woke up and came out.

I would cook. Yes. It wasn't the first time Luke had stayed at my place after a night out before, and I was always awake before him, so I cooked.

Never mind the fact I had a marching band in my head, and the thought of food made my stomach roll—I needed something hot and heavy and full of carbs and grease.

I pulled the ingredients from the cupboard to make pancakes from scratch and took bacon from the fridge. I busied myself making it, focusing on cooking instead of what had happened.

What I really needed to do was call Blaire, my lifelong best friend, and tell her how badly I'd screwed up. I couldn't do it while Luke was here, though, so my best option was to feed Luke and get rid of him as soon as humanly possible.

That was how you dealt with a man you wanted to get rid of, wasn't it? With food. And baggy sweatpants, greasy hair, and yesterday's mascara.

If that was true, I had it down. My hair was a dirty bun on top of my head with loose tendrils of stupid baby hairs hanging down around my ears and neck, and my mascara was doing a really good job of getting me ready to be a panda for Halloween this year.

As for the sweatpants... Well, that was the hangover uniform, wasn't it? Especially if you had company.

My bedroom door opened. "I smell food."

I turned around, a glass of water in hand, and look right at my naked best friend. "Luke! For the love of God! Put some pants on!"

He looked down. "Fuck!" He clasped his hands over his cock and ran back into my room, slamming the door behind him.

I got all of a flash of his tanned ass before the door shut, and that was enough to make me giggle.

Two minutes later, right as I flipped pancakes, he reappeared, wearing a pair of gray sweatpants and nothing much else.

There were times when I hated that he left clothes in my dresser. This was one of them.

Gray sweatpants were sexier than they had any right to be.

"You know," I said, flipping the last pancake. "If you need hangover clothes in my dresser, you need to drink less."

"You know," he shot back, sliding onto the stool at the island. "If it feels like you're screaming at me, you should greet me with aspirin and water."

"If it feels like I'm screaming at you, you should learn to control your alcohol intake." I slid a bottle of aspirin across the island at him. "Water in the fridge."

"I have to get my own water?"

"You drank your own shots of tequila, so yes. It's not like I'm standing here asking you to cook me a breakfast casserole. I'm making you food. Stop being a giant baby." I slid the pancakes onto a plate and checked the bacon. It was done, so I slid that onto another plate and set both on the island between us.

Luke pulled a bottle of water from the fridge. "You got any syrup?"

"How can you stomach syrup after fifty gallons of tequila?" I tugged a stool to the side and sat, not bothering with a plate of my own as I snagged a pancake and bacon and sandwiched them together to eat.

Look. I never claimed to be a lady.

I was wearing sweatpants and yesterday's t-shirt. I was a real girl, Pinocchio.

Maybe this was what Shania Twain was really singing about in her song. I felt like a woman. An awkward, mid-twenties woman in need of a face wipe and a shower, but a woman all the same.

After all, if your twenties didn't taste like regret, had you done it right at all?

The intelligent side of me said yes, you'd done it right if you hadn't been wrecked the entire time.

Not that I was that person. I worked in a bar—the very bar we'd staggered out of last night, actually. I saw more than my fair share of drunk people, but occasionally the tequila came out and then I was screwed.

Like Luke's aunt's wedding. The speeches were barely over, and his grandma was demanding shots of tequila on everyone's tables.

It was my Achille's heel.

His too, apparently.

"Syrup is heaven," Luke replied, retrieving it from the cupboard. "I will never be too hungover for syrup."

I grabbed my second piece of bacon and chewed on it. I didn't know how he could eat something so sweet, but then again, I wasn't exactly someone with a sweet tooth.

"Aren't you using a plate?" he asked, sitting back down.

"No." I grabbed another slice of bacon. "I'm too hungover for a plate."

"But not too hungover to cook."

"I'll throw the pancakes in the trash."

"Whoa, whoa, whoa, don't be hasty." He yanked the plate full of pancakes toward him. "So. Any ideas why I woke up naked?"

Great.

Here we go.

Play it cool, Aspen. Think on your toes.

I paused, a crispy rasher of bacon pinched between my finger and thumb. "You don't remember?"

He raised an eyebrow. "If I could remember, do you think I'd be asking?"

I lowered the bacon. "You really don't remember?"

Luke shook his head. "I didn't flash the building manager again, did I?"

It took everything I had to bite back a laugh at that memory. "No, and I think Mrs. Carmichael was very thankful for that. I'm not entirely sure she's over the last time."

"Thank God. So, what happened?"

"We got back here, and you decided you were wearing too many clothes to sleep in and stripped." I shrugged a shoulder, the bacon jigging with it. "Sorry. No juicy story, and no flashing anyone."

"Not even a stranger?"

"No. We were surprisingly well-behaved last night." Except for the part where we banged… If you could even call it that. It was somewhat of a stretch.

Luke drizzled syrup on his pancakes. And by drizzled, I meant drenched. "That sounds like the most boring Fourth of July ever."

"It was." I nodded. "Blaire didn't even have to flash anyone to get served at the bar this year."

"The last time Blaire flashed anyone at the bar to get served, she ended up breaking a guy's nose ten minutes later."

Ah. Yeah. That was true. No wonder my boss, Declan, had made sure she was served within minutes of her approaching the bar.

"He did deserve that," I reminded Luke. "I mean, she'd hadn't even gotten her nipples out. There was no need to try to kiss her tit."

"There was no need for Blaire to get them out. She could have exercised some patience."

"The only thing Blaire exercises is her mouth. When have you ever known her to have patience?"

Luke chewed on a piece of bacon, then tilted it in my direction in acknowledgment. "True. She has the patience of a toddler at snack time."

"How do you know how patient a toddler is at snack time?"

"I babysit for my cousin."

"You did that once."

"All right, whatever. I baby*sat*." He reached for my glass of juice and finished it, making me frown. "So nothing bad happened last night? For real?"

I met his blue eyes. "Don't you think I'd have told you if it did?"

No. Liar.

He considered that for a second, eating the rest of his slice of bacon, then shrugged and said, "Well, given that you bring up the time I swung my dick like a helicopter on my twenty-first birthday, I guess you would."

"Okay, but," I snorted, "That will be brought up to every girlfriend, at every party, and at every possible "embarrassing story time" until you die."

"Aspen, you once sat on the curb and had a conversation with a cat about squirrels."

"I'll have you know he was a great listener, thank you very much."

"Of course he was. He was a cat."

"Cats have a tendency to walk off and ignore you." I licked my fingers and grabbed my empty glass to refill it. Sharing a glass with him didn't seem like such a big deal after the whole saliva-swap thing last night. "A lot like you do."

"Only when you moan," he muttered, stabbing the final piece of pancake on his plate with a fork. "I have to admit, I'm real fuckin' surprised we managed to pull off a night out without either hurting ourselves, flashing someone, or doing something really stupid."

I sipped my juice and smiled. "Yeah, well, there's a first time for everything."

It just hadn't been last night.

"All right. You mind if I use your shower before I go?" He put his plate and fork in the sink.

"Since when have you ever asked to use my shower?"

"Good point." He smirked, chucking me under the chin before walking in the direction of my bathroom. "Thanks, Asp."

I raised my glass in response, tilting the top in his direction.

"YOU DID *WHAT?*" BLAIRE SHRIEKED, LUNGING forward and almost knocking over her wine glass.

The hair of the dog, all right? Plus, it was Friday night which meant girls' night in. You couldn't have girls' night without wine.

"I know," I whined, burying my face in my hands.

"You had sex with Luke?"

"It was an accident!" I peered at her over the tips of my fingers. "I swear. It just happened."

She quirked one eyebrow. "Yeah? What? Did he just trip and stick his erect penis into your vagina?"

"No, but he was uncomfortably close to sticking it in my ass."

Blaire held up one hand, her aqua manicure flashing as she did. "You're gonna need to go from the top. Wind back to the start."

I grabbed my wine glass and drained the rest of it, then settled back on the sofa and tugged a cushion onto my lap. Let's face it—I'd be burying my face into it in around two minutes.

"Okay. Well, we came back here, and I walked into the doorframe—"

"Of course you did. You barely knew what day of the week it was."

"Neither did you," I shot back. "Anyway, he lunged to stop me falling and…we kissed."

Blaire blinked, her caramel-colored eyes shining with amusement. "Just like that? It just happened?"

"That's how I remember it."

"All right. Carry on. I can't wait for this."

I could. I never wanted to relive last night again. "I don't really know what happened after that except I walked into the dresser. Apparently, tequila means you misjudge distance. Who knew?"

"The Mexicans. For a long time. And now they laugh at us idiots."

Having been to many of Luke's family events, I knew that much was true. "Anyway—he helped me to the bed and checked my hip. Then I kissed him."

"You kissed him?"

"What? I didn't mean to!"

"There's a lot of that going on in this story," Blaire said dryly, leaning over to top up our glasses with the last of the wine in the bottle.

I flipped her the bird and continued. "One thing led to another, and after some kissing and stuff, we…did it."

I really didn't want to go into any more depth than that.

"Did he try to put it in your ass before or after?" She passed me my glass and sat back, cradling hers.

"Before. And when I told him, he said, 'whoops.'"

"Whoops?" Her eyes bugged. "Yeah, he's never had anyone put anything in his ass by accident."

"Unless there's something he's not telling us, I highly doubt he has," I replied. "So, yeah. That's it. We did it."

"Just like that?" She blinked at me. "Well, how was it? What happened this morning? What happens now?"

I said nothing.

"Don't look at me like I just asked you to uncover the meaning of life. You boned your best friend. Or, rather, he boned you. That's not exactly something you do every day."

I took a deep breath. "I don't know what happens. It was…"

She leaned forward, grinning. "Amazing? Mind-blowing? Something you have to do again? I have to admit, I definitely have Luke in the best-sex-of-your-life bracket in my imagination."

"Uh…not exactly."

She paused.

"It was awful, Blaire. So bad. I've never had sex so bad in my entire life."

Her eyes widened. "Worse than Ross?"

I nodded. "Worse than Ross."

"How bad is bad?"

"Tap-tap-squirt."

She gasped, clasping her hand over her mouth. "No! Not Luke!"

"Yep."

"Was it the tequila?"

"I don't know, but I can't exactly bring it up, can I?" I held out my hands. "He wandered into the kitchen this morning with no recollection of what happened last night. Despite the fact I wanted to fry myself with the bacon, it was totally normal. I genuinely think he can't remember."

Blaire stared at me. She didn't even move for a second, but when she did, it was to bring her other hand up to her mouth, still clasping her wine glass. "He didn't remember?"

"Nope. And if he did, he obviously didn't want to bring it up. Not that I blame him."

"You didn't come at all?"

"Only to Misery Town, but I'm pretty sure my train is going to take me on to Awkwardville."

"Well, shit." My best friend sagged back against the sofa. "I feel like he'd tell you if he remembered. If only so you can sweep it under the rug and never talk about it again."

"Same. I just… I don't want to tell him if he doesn't remember it."

"Why not?"

"What the fuck am I supposed to say? 'Hey, bestie! I just wanted to let you know that we drunkenly screwed last night, but you're the worst I've ever had. Hope this isn't awkward!'"

Blaire paused. "I'd send it."

"Of course you would. But I'm not you." I twirled my glass by the stem. "I can't tell him that, Blaire. I'm pretty sure it'll wreck our friendship."

"More than your two minutes of Heaven?"

"Two minutes might be pushing it."

"Wow. Okay. So, you're just going to ignore it and hope you forget about it?"

I sighed and shrugged one shoulder. "I guess so. He doesn't remember, so telling him what happened and potentially embarrassing him isn't going to do either of us any good. I'd rather ignore that it ever happened and keep my best friend, no matter how awkward that might be."

Blaire rocked her head from side to side, then shrugged in something that looked an awful lot like a reluctant agreement. Understanding, at the very least. "I get it, but you've been best friends since you were five. When I moved here, it was like getting blood from a stone to be your friend at first."

I snorted. True. Luke and I had been attached at the hip as long as I could remember.

"I just… I get what you're saying, Asp, but I think you should think about telling him what happened. Do you really want to keep a secret from him?"

"I never told him you made out with his cousin."

She held up one finger. "Not important."

"Totally important."

"No, I don't think it is." She shook her head emphatically, her almost-black curls swinging from side to side. "That's my secret, not yours."

"I saw you kissing him so hard I wondered who had the game in that set of tonsil tennis."

"Still not important." She waved me off. "You had sex with him, Aspen."

"Do you call that sex? I call that a drunken mistake that nobody should ever remember in their life."

She sighed. "Okay. I guess then your question is: are you one hundred percent certain Luke doesn't remember what you did last night?"

I nodded firmly. "I'm one hundred percent certain that Luke doesn't remember. I just know he doesn't."

THREE

LUKE

What Not To Do After Tequila

I HAD A LONG LIST OF THINGS YOU SHOULD never, ever fucking do after tequila.

Flash an old lady.

Strip naked in the public park.

Allow your abs to be used as a body shot platform for a bachelorette party.

Your best friend.

And if I had to pick one of those things to never do again after tequila, it would one hundred percent be the last thing.

'Cause, fuck.

Just *fuck*.

I had no idea what I'd been thinking last night. Having sex with Aspen? There was no possible way that could not go wrong after the amount we'd drunk.

My family was a fucking nightmare at holidays, and even though most of them weren't even American, they used every possible holiday as an excuse to drink tequila. Fourth of July included. I was almost certain they'd cleaned the bar out after we'd left if the four-a.m. text from my cousin was anything to go by.

But me—shit.

I'd been so stupid. So, so stupid. Kissing her had been one thing, but having sex with her? And fucking it up the way I had?

Jesus. There was no way I could tell her I knew what had happened last night. The only saving grace I had was that she didn't seem to remember a thing. We'd known each other long enough that one of us could have brought it up if we both remembered, so I guess there was that.

She would never know how the worst two minutes of my life had been with her.

Not that she was bad. Holy shit, no. She wasn't. She was my best friend, but she was hot as fuck. I'd have to be blind not to be attracted to her.

But of all the nights to do something about those damn honey-colored eyes and a mouth with a smile so powerful it could light up an entire town, it had to be last night.

It had to be after a stupid number of tequila shots. A stupid number of lines of salt licked off the back of my hand. A stupid number of lime slices sucked between my lips.

Of course it did.

And it had to be a terrible, horrible, awkward two minutes of her being too drunk to even fake an orgasm accurately.

And then, this morning, when I'd asked her why I was butt naked—not that I'd even realized until I'd strolled into her kitchen and she'd screamed at me—she'd come up with a perfectly good excuse as to why I was naked.

At first, I'd thought she was lying. She was covering up the truth. Who the fuck wanted to admit that the worst sex of their life had been with their best friend? It was like telling your old dog that you preferred your new puppy.

Kinda.

But no, the more I probed, the more she insisted I'd stripped off. Which, to be honest, I had a record of when drunk. I wasn't exactly a stand-up member of society after a few drinks, but at least I'd never punched anyone or been arrested.

I was just, you know… Free.

How the fuck was I supposed to tell Aspen what had happened? That we'd had what barely passed as sex and she'd faked it to make me feel good?

Like I didn't know that a woman couldn't come in two minutes of thrusting.

I wasn't fifteen. I was twenty-five. Not that it made a difference last night.

Nope. That was all on tequila.

The bruise on my right ankle? Tequila.

The knock to my ego? Tequila.

The shame of pumping and dumping my best friend?

Te. Fucking. Quila.

The worst part of this situation with Aspen was that I had no fucking idea what to do now. I couldn't bring it up. I remembered the night clearly, and she'd been willing in every single thing we'd done—which wasn't a damn lot— but still.

What if she didn't believe me? What if she thought I'd taken advantage of her? I'd never do that. Not to her or anyone else.

We'd both drunk the exact same amount. We'd both managed to pile into a cab and go back to her place simply because it was closest.

That was how it worked. She left hangover clothes in my bottom drawer, and I left them in hers.

She was just much better at cooking the next day than I was.

But, fuck. How did we move forward from this? Did I sit here on my sofa eating Doritos and pretend it never happened? Was that for the best? How the hell were you supposed to apologize to your best friend for screwing her out of, well, a damn good screw?

At least I knew she'd slept well. She snored like a harbor setting off an alarm to bring a boat in safely.

God fucking knows I'd prodded her to roll over and shut up enough times last night.

Shit, though. Shit.

I leaned forward and ran one hand through my hair. The other was covered in orange dust from the Doritos I'd been eating, and when I sat back, I licked my fingers clean.

Then I scratched my balls.

Look. I was hungover, tormented, and I'd put fifty bucks on the line betting that I'd fucked up my relationship with my best friend.

If I wanted to lick Dorito dust off my hand and scratch my balls with the other while feeling sorry for myself, then I'd fucking well do it.

The truth was, I had no idea what to do with this situation. There was hardly a handbook for what to do after having bad sex with your best friend.

And there should have been.

This was way more valuable than algebra, and I was basically an expert in that.

Or I was. I hadn't used it for seven years.

Who said school was useful?

I tossed the empty packet of Doritos to the side and focused on the TV. The credits for American Pickers blinked off the screen, but I really didn't care what Frank and Mike were doing tonight.

Nope.

All I could picture in my head was my best friend.

Aspen. Dark hair. Honey eyes. Full lips. A smile brighter than LED lights on a Christmas tree.

Perhaps the weirdest way I'd ever referred to a woman's smile, but effective all the same.

Fuck. She was my best friend.

We'd made sandcastles together in Kindergarten—and she'd hit me with her spade, cementing our friendship for life.

I'd stuck up for her in second grade when she'd forgotten she was wearing a skirt on the monkey bars and accidentally flashed the entire playground.

She'd pulled a girl's hair in fourth grade when she'd been mean to me.

Sixth grade had brought puberty for us both, and I'd given her my sweater when someone had stolen her training bra.

Ninth grade had come with a cheating asshole who'd taken her for granted—and my fist cracking his nose.

Twelfth grade had come with prom, where I'd asked her before I'd considered asking anyone else. She'd said yes, and we'd spent the night with our friends, secretly drinking and laughing our asses off the entire night.

No, fuck. I couldn't lose her.

I couldn't ever tell her what had happened last night.

I couldn't ever sit in front of her and tell her the truth, not if she didn't remember. If she had genuinely forgotten about that disaster, then good for her. I wished I could.

I wished I could wipe the memory of what we'd done. Not knowing that it had happened was definitely preferable.

Yep.

It was that simple. Last night had to remain a secret.

At all costs.

"IF YOU KEPT YOUR FRIDGE PROPERLY stocked, you wouldn't need to raid mine." Aspen flicked her golden-brown hair over her shoulder. It was a mess of waves and straightness, and I knew she'd gone to bed with wet hair.

"I just haven't been to the store yet," I said, pulling the cream cheese from her fridge. "Do you have bagels?"

"Yeah. Do you even have bread?"

"It might not be edible, but I have some." I wasn't actually sure. Maybe I did, maybe I didn't. "Can I have a bagel?"

"There is zero point in me answering that question."

She pulled her coffee cup from under the machine and took the milk off the island. "You're going to take two no matter what I say."

Laughing, I grabbed the bagel packet and pulled two out. "At least I'm not asking you to make them for me."

"Yeah, well, you're cleaning up your mess."

"I have to be at work in an hour!"

"Luke." She spun around and fixed me with her honey eyes. "If you cannot make, eat, and clean up after yourself and get to work in an hour, then you need to move back in with your mom."

"Hard pass." I cut the bagels in half. "Not as long as my grandma is living there."

Aspen shuddered. "I wouldn't want to live with her either."

"Why? Because she'll force-feed you tequila?"

"I've had enough tequila to last me a lifetime," she replied shortly.

"Until your birthday next weekend."

"I'm not drinking on my birthday. I'm going to be a responsible adult, stay in, and watch a movie."

"Have you told Blaire that yet?"

She paused. "No, but…"

I laughed, putting one bagel into the toaster. "Please let me be there when you do that."

"You know, I can stop you coming in here and eating

my food any time I want."

"I have a spare key."

"I'll change the lock."

"And you'll give me another key because you lose just about everything that's smaller than your cell phone. Not that your phone is even safe from being lost itself…"

"One time, Luke. One time."

"Maybe one time a month."

"That's it." She darted toward me and pulled my just-popped bagel from the toaster before I had to get it. "This is mine. Thanks for making me breakfast."

I glared at her, but she ignored me, choosing to take the cream cheese and slather a thick layer on one side of the bagel. She put the top on it then bit into it, grinning at me with a smear of cheese on her cheek.

"You even eat like a two-year-old," I said, putting the other bagel in.

"And you eat like a fifteen-year-old boy in perpetual puberty," she shot back. "And you cost me a fortune. No wonder you have more money than me. You eat all mine."

Sadly accurate. "That's how it works when you're best friends. I eat all your money, and then you drink mine."

"Not anymore. I'm quitting drinking."

"Sure you are, Asp. Just like you did after your twenty-first."

"Oh my God, I totally quit drinking."

I choked on my coffee. "For two weeks!"

"I still quit!" She laughed, finally wiping the cheese from her face. "Just because I started again doesn't mean I didn't quit. But I mean it this time. I think I'm still hungover from Saturday. I can't do it anymore. I'm getting too old for it."

This time, I was able to get my damn bagel before she took it. "You're going to be twenty-five, not seventy-five."

"That's a whole quarter of a century. Assuming I won't even live to one hundred, I've already lived more than a quarter of my life."

"You won't make it to twenty-five if you don't stop that shit."

"You could never kill me. You love me way too much."

The bite of bagel I'd just taken went straight to the back of my mouth, blocking my throat. I choked, smacking my fist against my chest. It was well and truly fucking stuck, and the next thing I felt was a huge whack between my shoulder blades.

The lodged piece of bagel coughed up into my hand, and I tossed it into the sink.

"If you're going to die, could you not do it in my apartment? I don't think my insurance covers my best friend choking himself to death." Aspen squeezed my arm. "And when you can breathe again, please remove your spit-food from my sink."

"It's so nice to see you care so much about me," I drawled, taking the bottle of water she offered you.

"I just saved your life. It wasn't Casper the friendly ghost who punched you in the back."

"You punched me in the back?"

"Well, you punching yourself in the chest wasn't working. I figured if we both did it at the same time, the air in your body would push the food out." She shrugged and leaned against the counter, cradling her coffee. "Worked, didn't it?"

I nodded, standing up straight. "Or you could have just done the Heimlich."

Aspen rolled her eyes. "The correct thing to say is 'thank you for saving my life.'"

"Thank you for saving my life," I replied, grinning.

She glared at me until I pulled her into a one-arm hug. She stiffened, only relaxing when I let her go, but given that she'd been in a shitty mood ever since I'd shown up this morning...

"I should go," I said, stepping back from her. "Before I almost kill myself again. I'd hate to be an issue with your insurance company."

She snorted. "More like your ego couldn't survive me having to save your ass again."

"Ah, how well you know me." I winked and stuffed my phone in my pocket. "When do you start work?"

"Four. Are you coming in?"

"Probably. I think Justin has a crush on you."

She wrinkled her face up and shoved me. "Get your spit-food out of my sink and take your bullshit with you."

I laughed, scooping out the food I'd choked up, and made sure to drop it in the trash on my way out of the door.

Something smashed, and the sound of Aspen cursing the air blue followed me as I walked away.

Man, she was in a dreadful mood.

FOUR

ASPEN

Fuck yourself, Aunt Flo

I THREW THE BAR CLOTH DOWN WITH A HUFF. The bar had been open for the evening for forty-five minutes, and I'd already had to diffuse one fight and throw one person out before another started.

It was four-forty-five.

That's right. Clearly, some people were abiding by the rule that it was five o'clock somewhere. Don't get me wrong, that was my favorite rule ever. I believed that everyone should indulge in "It's Five O'Clock Somewhere" at some point in their life.

But that day was not the first day of my period.

No, siree. Today was not the day to fuck with me. My hormones were raging, I was bleeding more than any human should have been able to without passing out, and my uterus had a miniature wolverine inside it trying to claw its way out.

And Aunt Flo, the raging bitch, had caught me off-guard, ten minutes into my shift.

I should have known. I'd been grumpy as fuck all day, especially this morning. Although I'd put that down to the fact Luke was eating my food, and I wanted to eat my food. All of it. Alone. In the middle of my floor without any pants on.

Yep. That really should have been my first clue that the unwanted aunt was making a visit.

Usually, given that this was Texas, I was the first person to complain that I was required to wear black pants to work behind the bar. Today, I was thankful.

Black pants hid a multitude of sins.

Like uncomfortably large sanitary pads from the ladies' room dispenser.

I kept my eye on the clock as it crept closer to five o'clock. Not only was I waiting for Blaire to save my ass and drop me a tampon on her way home from the lawyer's office she worked on, but I was also waiting on Luke and his band of merry builders to traipse their dust all over my clean floor.

And his stupid friend, Justin, who was more handsy than a toddler after the cookie jar. I didn't care if he had a crush on me. I'd long suspected that he had, but he was also kind of a jerk, and I'd dated more than enough of those in high school.

And in college.

And since then.

And there were more than enough of those sending me dick pics on dating apps.

But I digress.

I waved goodbye to Mr. Gomez, a regular who came in at four-fifteen on the dot every single day. He worked down at the surf shop on the beach which was just a stone's throw from the bar. He lived a couple blocks back from here, so every day, he stopped in, bought one double gin and tonic in a pint glass, and read the paper.

That was the fun part about where I worked. It was the perfect hangout for both regulars and tourists and those who stopped in for a night out every now and then.

I mean, nightlife wasn't exactly popping in Port Wynne, Texas.

The only thing that was was the Mexican food, and that was because Luke's grandmother was the Gordon Ramsey of Mexico.

Complete with every other word being a profanity.

She was simultaneously adorable and utterly fucking terrifying.

I took a deep breath as the doors to the bar opened, and five tall, young, muscular men walked in. Luke Taylor was the first, with the other four flanking him like they were some ridiculous boyband appearing on stage for a concert or something.

One Direction, eat your heart out.

Well, they'd have to if they were still a thing.

Luke's face lit up as soon as he saw me, and he grinned wide, his bright blue eyes sparkling. "Hey. How's your day been?"

Great. I started bleeding from my vagina, I don't have any chocolate here, and now I have to handle your buddies here.

"Aside from having to break up a fight and kick someone out with the help of Mr. Gomez, great," I replied. "Yours?"

"Well, Sean resisted the urge to catcall random women today after the boss choked him on his own balls, so not bad." His eyes twinkled a little brighter.

"You guys want your usual?" I scanned Luke and his workmates.

Five nods answered me.

"Does the usual come with your number?" Justin asked as I turned and pulled two glasses down from the shelf.

I set both glasses on the bar, then reached down and pulled my black ballet flat from my foot and held it up. "No, but it comes with this around the back of your head if you don't drop it."

He chuckled. "Whoa—calm down. You on your period

or something?"

My shoe slapped against the tiled floor when I dropped it. I leveled my eyes at him, my glare meeting his cocky, entitled stare. "I'm sorry, I wasn't aware that the current state of my uterus was any of your business."

"Justin," Luke warned. "Get off her back."

Then, Blaire appeared behind Justin and smacked the back of his head with a resounding *thwack*.

"Shit!" Justin ducked, rubbing his head as he turned. "The fuck was that for?"

"If you don't know, then I got another for you." She wriggled her fingers with a dark glare and turned to me. "You want me to throw him out? He's all muscle and no strength like those pretty boys on Instagram."

Justin bristled. "You want me to prove you wrong?"

"Boy, you try provin' me wrong, and you're gonna find my heel so far up your ass that doctors are gonna be extracting it for a week." She flicked the side of his head. "Now shut up before I make you."

Like he stood a chance to prove her wrong. Blaire was happily spoken for and had been for two years. She was just a little eccentric.

I shot her a grateful smile, then one to Luke, and got to pulling their beers. They chatted amongst themselves as I did that, and I took money from each of them to pay for their drinks.

When they were dealt with, Blaire nodded me off to the side and discreetly handed me a small, fabric pouch covered with unicorns.

"Thank you," I whispered, squeezing her hand. "You just saved my life."

"And Justin's." She grinned.

"And Justin's," I agreed. "You going to Tom's?"

She nodded. "He's finally back from Michigan. Text me if you need anything, okay?"

"Will do. Thank you." I hugged her quickly and retook my place back behind the bar. I tucked the little pouch beneath the bar, ignoring Luke's questioning eyebrow raise. "So, Mack, how's Daisy?"

The new dad grinned wide. "Keeping me up all damn night and looking cute as she does it."

"Whipped by a three-week-old," Justin muttered.

Blaire whacked him around the back of the head as she walked past. "Don't worry, Mack, I got it for you."

"Thanks, B."

"Anytime." She grinned and waved as she left.

"She's a bitch," Justin said, rubbing the back of his head.

Luke side-eyed him. "Maybe if you weren't a fucking prick every time you opened your mouth, she wouldn't have to beat a hundred brain cells out of you every day."

"He never had that many to begin with," I interjected.

"Maybe when he was born, but he's been hit so many times he forgets to use the brain cells he has left before he opens his mouth."

Luke snorted—and so did Mack, Sean, and Will. Justin looked like I'd kicked his puppy.

That was what he got for asking me if I was on my period.

I didn't ask him what his sperm count was, did I?

My uterus, my business.

"Would it be so hard for you to be nice to me?" Justin asked me.

"Would it be so hard for you to not hit on me every time we're in the same room?" I shot back before I moved to the young woman waiting to order. I poured the two glasses of wine she wanted and added it to her tab before returning to the guys.

"She has a point," Luke says. "She's told you she's not interested a thousand times. If we were in high school, I'd be breaking your nose for bugging her this much."

"You should still be doing that." I pulled my glass of water from beneath the bar. "It's in the friend code."

"The friend code?" Will snorted. "I don't know why y'all never dated."

I choked on my water.

"Wow," Luke said. "Is the idea that abhorrent to you?"

I flipped him the bird and put the glass down. "We

never dated because, well, no." I shrugged at Will. "We're best friends. I can't think of any situation where we'd ever want to date each other."

But tequila will have you screw each other.

Will looked between us. "I always pegged you for secretly fucking each other."

Now, it was Justin who coughed on his drink.

Was there something in the air today?

"Definitely not," I said firmly. "Never have, never will."

Except for Saturday night.

Luke smirked and held out one hand. "You heard her. Besides, it's not like she can handle me."

I rested my hand on my hip and cocked it out. "I couldn't handle you? Who do you peg yourself for? Some hotshot porn star?"

"Maybe I do."

"Luke, you almost killed yourself on a mouthful of bagel this morning. You're hardly going to blow my mind in bed if you can't even eat a bagel without choking." *Or, you know, I mean, in general, apparently…*

"Choking on a bagel and having sex are two different things," he said.

I snorted and put my glass back under the bar. "I should damn well hope so. If not, I have an awful lot of questions."

"Yeah," Justin piped up. "The only thing you should choke on is—"

"Finish that sentence, and you'll be choking on my fist," I snapped at him, pointing my finger at his face. "I dare you."

Justin said nothing, instead choosing to flip me his middle finger and disappear to the bathrooms.

Mack grinned. "Always a pleasure to see him shut up."

"More of a pleasure to see him leave," I muttered, grabbing a cloth and wiping up a spill on the other end of the bar.

They all laughed.

At least we weren't talking about me having sex with Luke anymore.

"All right, question," Sean said, leaning forward on the bar. He was leaner than his friends, but his arms were still as toned as theirs. "If you had to pick right now between me, Will, and Luke, who would you take home?"

I stilled. What the hell kinda question was that? "I'm too sober for Truth or Dare."

"Weren't you giving up drinking?" Luke smirked.

"I was until y'all walked in here," I replied. "You'd drive nuns to drink."

"I'd consider that a personal triumph." Will's brown eyes shone with laughter. "Well, who'd you pick?"

I didn't even need to think about it. "Mack."

"Mack wasn't an option."

"I know that, but he'd bring Daisy, then I'd get baby snuggles." I shrugged. "Luke would just eat all my food like he does anyway. Sean, you'd try to perv me in the shower, and Will, don't take this the wrong way, but I'm not a blonde kinda girl."

He laughed. "I know that. Honestly, Daisy aside, I thought you'd pick Luke."

"So did I," Sean agreed. "As much as it kills me."

I rolled my eyes. "Please. He already invites himself into my apartment and eats all my food. It doesn't matter if I'd take him home or not—he shows up whenever he pleases."

"That's why I thought you'd pick him." Will shrugged. "You're halfway to dating. Are y'all sure you haven't kissed?"

Yes. We have. A lot.

I raised my eyebrows and, with a tiny snort, looked at Luke. His expression was as disbelieving as mine was, except his lips were curved to one side with the tiniest hint of amusement at the suggestion. "Absolutely sure we've never kissed," I lied smoothly.

Luke nodded. "Not once. Well, there was that awkward almost-kiss at prom, but that was idiot here turning her head the wrong way for the photos."

"Me? You moved, too!" I jabbed my finger at him across the bar. "It was a freak accident, and technically not a kiss. Stop saying it was."

"Did your lips touch?" Sean asked, looking between us.

"No."

"Yes."

I glared at Luke. "They did not touch!"

He held his hands up. "Just saying it as I remember it."

"More like how you dreamed it." I poked my tongue out at him and walked down the bar to where Mr. and Mrs. Sanderson were waiting.

They came in every night like clockwork for two glasses of Merlot each.

I served them their first and set them up on tabs then, once again, went back to the guys. "Justin still not back?"

"Nah, you probably bruised his ego a little too much this time." Luke shrugged.

"Just as well," Sean added. "That way he didn't have to hear about you two kissing."

"We didn't kiss!" I pointed my finger at him, then slowly moved it side to side until I'd pointed at all four guys. "Got it?"

"Who didn't kiss?" Justin came back right at that moment.

"Nobody," Mack said quickly, winking at me. "You leaving?"

He nodded, taking two big drinks of his beer until it was almost empty. "Savannah called."

"Who's Savannah?" I asked.

Justin turned his attention to me. "Why? You jealous?"

"Greener than a field of grass in the middle of summer," I replied dryly.

"She's his fuck buddy." Luke's lips twitched. "Not exactly anything to be jealous of."

"At least I have a fuck buddy," Justin drawled, shrugging his jacket on.

"Yeah, that's what I want," Luke replied. "A fuck buddy. Someone who'll call and use me when they've got an itch to scratch."

"You say that like it's a bad thing." Justin grinned and, with a wave goodbye, left.

I shook my head and took his glass. "I don't know how y'all put up with him."

"He's not wrong." Will laughed. "I'd take a fuck buddy. Hey, Aspen, you seein' anyone?"

"You'll be seeing your maker if you carry on with that crap, William." I laughed myself as I put the dirty glass in the tray beneath the bar to take to the back. "No wonder Mack's the only one of y'all with a girlfriend. He's the only one with a half-decent bone in his body."

"Yeah, don't you remember that time I hit on before I met her?" Mack asked with a chuckle.

"Yes, but you said please. These morons just take it for granted that I'll date them."

Luke mock-gasped, touching his hand to his chest right as I turned around. "I've never done such a thing."

I gripped the edge of the bar and, leaning forward, twisted my lips into a half smile. "You don't need to. You take it for granted that I'll always have food in my kitchen."

"And yet, you still go shopping." He held his hands out to the sides.

"If she didn't, you'd fuckin' starve, you lazy bastard." Sean laughed, causing the other guys to, too.

"Nah, I'd call Abuelita and get her to cook for me." Luke grinned.

"Then you'd weigh three-hundred pounds in a year," I reminded him. "She'd feed the entire homeless population of the United States if anyone would give her access to a kitchen big enough."

"And people skilled enough," Will added. "I remember, one time, when we were fifteen, I asked her if she needed help in the kitchen. She told me in no uncertain terms that if I couldn't speak Spanish, I needed to get the fuck out of her kitchen immediately."

I almost choked on my water. "Been there. Nobody offers Maria Lòpez help unless she asks you for it first."

"And even then, you verify what she wants the help for." Luke shook his head. "Still, she'd cook three meals a day for me if I asked her."

"Nana's boy." I grinned and swiped two empty wine

glasses from the bar, waving goodbye to the couple they'd belonged to.

"Whatever. You don't complain when she sends me to your place with take-out containers full of food."

"Obviously not. Her food tastes like magic. I'll take all the food I can get from her." I put the dirty glasses into the tray and, after skimming the bar quickly, took Will's empty glass to refill it. "In fact, bringing me her food is the least you can do after the amount of mine you eat."

He moved his hand in a motion that said I was talking too much and muttered under his breath like when we were kids.

I shot him a look as I slid Will his beer.

Luke sighed. "Fine. I'll call her and tell her I ate all your food again."

I grinned. "Damn right you will."

FIVE
ASPEN

Let's Not Taco 'Bout That

TUESDAY.

Three days post worst-ever-sex, and Blaire wouldn't shut up about it. She still couldn't understand why I didn't want to bring it up to Luke, and I was *this-fucking-close* to blocking her number.

It wasn't going to happen. It was as simple as that.

If the last three days had shown me anything, it was that our friendship could move on as normal. Saturday night hadn't been mentioned once or even referred to by anyone.

What had happened between us was done. It was in the past. And, for some weird reason, nothing had changed between us. I'm sure it would be different if Luke remembered, but I wasn't going to jeopardize anything by telling him it.

I mean, come on.

Nothing good could come from telling my best friend he was the worst guy I'd ever slept with.

And yes, I was sure the tequila had a hand in that, but I didn't want to know what it would be like to have sex with him while sober.

I was pretty sure I didn't.

Mostly.

I think.

All right, I wanted to know. I was a curious person. I liked having answers, which was why I could never become a physicist. There were too many questions and not enough answers.

Also, I was bad at science.

Right now, for me, 'What was Luke like in bed while sober?' was right up there with 'Did aliens exist?"

Damn him. Damn him for being so drunk he couldn't remember. Damn me for not being drunk enough to forget.

If he remembered, if we could talk freely about it, then maybe the real thing would be a possibility.

You know. For the purpose of science. And curiosity.

Mostly curiosity.

Totally curiosity.

Damn it. I wasn't supposed to be thinking these things.

Luke was my best friend—not some weird fling. I was supposed to be wondering when he was bringing the enchiladas and quesadillas his grandma promised she'd make me.

I was supposed to wonder if he'd sit through another round of re-runs of The Big Bang Theory during dinner... Or if it was acceptable to ask him to bring me chocolate and tampons.

The chocolate? For sure. The tampons?

Ehhhhh.

I wasn't sure about that. Was that normal?

Not that it really mattered. I was almost out of options.

I had no tampons.

No sanitary towels.

And I was sitting on the toilet.

Which was why I was pondering the possibility of sleeping with my best friend without being under the influence of tequila.

Hormones. They were persnickety little fuckers.

They also needed to shut their bitch ass mouths.

See? Hormones? Problematic.

Ugh. Unless I wanted to run halfway across town with tissue stuck between my legs, I had no choice. Blaire was at work, and my parents were visiting friends in Austin.

I had to text Luke.

I sighed and picked my phone up from the mat on the floor.

ME: DEFCON FIVE EMERGENCY

What could I say? Drama was my friend, and Luke loved me for it. That and my full fridge.

LUKE: Who do I need to kill?

ME: Why do you always think you need to kill someone?

LUKE: You're a moody bitch this week, and there's a Defcon 5 emergency. Two and two equal four.

ME: You don't need to kill anyone.

LUKE: K, I'll grab my spade to bury the body.

I snorted.

Not a thing a girl should do while on her period and sitting on the toilet.

Bodies were gross.

I clenched my legs together as much as I possibly could, trying to ignore the vaginal-sneeze that proved I had no business leaving this bathroom until I had appropriate sanitary products.

ME: No bodies. Maybe yours if you don't bring me Abuelita's food anytime soon.

LUKE: I'll call her. Was that the Defcon 5?

ME: No.

LUKE: Then what do you want?

ME: I'm out of tampons.

Silence.

LUKE: And what the hell do you want me to do about that?

ME: I'm out of tampons. And I'm sitting on the toilet.

LUKE: Didn't you once tell Blaire her backup tampons needed a backup?

ME: Yes. I used the backups. Help me.

LUKE: I'm not cut out to buy tampons. This isn't okay.

ME: OMG PLEAAAASSSSEEEEEEE

ME: I NEEDS THEM

ME: I AM GOING TO CRY

LUKE: You're not going to cry over tampons.

True. I wasn't. But I was starting to get pins and needles in my legs from sitting on this toilet for so long, and that would make me cry.

ME: Please. I promise not to bitch at you for eating my food for one whole week.

LUKE: Oh, boy, push the boat out there, Asp.

ME: Please. Please. Please. Please.

LUKE: I'm sighing at you right now. You're lucky I'm on my lunch break.

ME: I'll even pay you back for your lunch.

LUKE: You'll make me lunch for my inevitable embarrassment. What do I need to buy?

I grabbed the empty tampon box and snapped a picture, then attached it to another message and sent it.

LUKE: What if they don't have those?

ME: Deal with that when you get there. Right now, I'm bleeding out while you argue semantics.

LUKE: If you were bleeding out, my life would be a lot more peaceful.

ME: I'm going to spit in your sandwich.

LUKE: Leaving now. Give me 10 minutes.

The way to a man's heart was definitely through his stomach.

It worked well to get your own way, too.

If someone had told teen me that, those years would have been a hell of a lot easier.

"ASPEN?" LUKE'S SHOUT FILTERED ITS WAY through to me in the bathroom.

"In the bathroom!"

"Still? Are you taking the world's biggest shit?"

"No, I'm saving the planet by bleeding directly into the toilet bowl!" I yelled. "Get in here and give me the damn tampons!"

There was a small knock on the door, then nothing. "You want me to come in there? Why can't you come and get it?"

"If I have to repeat about the bleeding again…"

"No! No! That's enough of that!" he said quickly. "Are you covered? For, you know, your dignity."

"My dignity went to shit when I got caught almost having sex with Simon Jones in the back seat of his car," I reminded him. "Hold on." I reached over to the towel rail and pulled a towel off, then used it to cover my body. "Okay. Come in."

The door handle creaked. Slowly, the door eked open, and Luke's face appeared. Well, his head appeared. His face was hidden behind his hand.

"Seriously. I'm not standing here performing a witch dance. Give me the damn tampons."

He parted his fingers and peeked through them. "Thank you. I don't need to see this."

I rolled my eyes and took the box from him. "It's a period, not a massacre."

"So why the Defcon five?"

"Because if you didn't bring the tampons, it'd be *your* massacre." I grinned and clutched the towel harder. "Now scoot. I'll be there in a sec to feed your fat ass."

He laughed, running out of the bathroom faster than I'd ever seen him run before.

The door clicked shut behind him—banged, actually—and I breathed a sigh of relief as I tore open the box.

Thank God.

A few minutes later, all was right again in my world, if you didn't count the fact that my legs were half dead from a ridiculous amount of time spent on the toilet.

"You washed your hands, right?" Luke eyed me as I joined him in the kitchen.

"No," I said slowly. "I make a habit of inserting things into my vagina and not washing my hands after."

"I can make my own sandwich." He moved to pass me.

I nudged him with my elbow. "Sit down. I'll make you a sandwich. Thank you, by the way. I really appreciate it."

He grunted and sat at the island. "So you should. That was a nightmare. Have you ever walked into a store and had to ask where the lady section is?"

I paused, my grip on the fridge door firm, and turned to him. I simply blinked. I wasn't going to justify that with an answer.

"It took three people before a poor woman at the customer service desk took pity on me and walked me to the tampon aisle," he went on, oblivious to my death stare. "She hovered over me for a second, and I started fucking sweating, Aspen. Sweating."

I bit my lip and moved the ingredients for his sandwich over to the board on the island.

"I almost dropped my phone trying to find the photo you sent me, and when I finally brought it up, I was so fucking confused I stood there like a lame damn duck for five minutes before she came back to help me like she knew I was a total idiot."

Was it wrong that I was way more amused about this than anything else? A part of me told me I should feel bad, but…

"Did you know there are tons of those things? The boxes are all different. There are different brands. Different sizes. Different… absorbency levels." He shuddered, his wide, muscled shoulders shaking with his cringey thought. "For flows and stuff."

"I shop there regularly. I am aware."

"Not that fucking regularly if you sent me to buy them," he muttered. "Anyway, the nice lady who was trying her best not to laugh at the idiot in the sanitary products aisle asked me who I was buying them for. My mom, my sister, my girlfriend…"

I chopped the lettuce.

"When I told her it was for my best friend, she looked

at me funny for a minute before nodding. Then, she dragged me over to the aisle with the candy and told me that Twizzlers went well with tampons. I was so confused I didn't question her, so here." He lifted a small bag from the stool next to him and tossed it in my direction. "You're the proud owner of eight packets of Twizzlers."

"Oooh, Twizzlers!" I dropped the knife and dove into the bag, pulling out all the long, red packets. "This is like heaven!"

"Dude." Luke leaned forward and held his hands out. "My sandwich?"

"Geez, who's on their period? You or me?" I put the candy down and went back to making his sandwich. "You should have saved the Twizzlers until after you got your food."

"Rookie mistake." He shook his head. "Please don't ever ask me to buy you tampons again. I'm not sure my ego or reputation can take it."

"Your reputation got shot to shit on your twenty-first when you mooned the mayor in the town square," I reminded him.

"And I haven't mooned anyone since," he replied. "My pants now stay firmly on when I drink."

Except for Saturday night.

I cleared my throat, focusing on the tomato I was cutting up. "Yeah, well, I think that's for the best for everyone."

"It's not my fault. I didn't wear pants at home until I was eight. This is on my parents. It's hard-wired in me to be pantsless."

"There's pantsless; then there's naked." I assembled the sandwich and cut it on two. "I'm sure there would have been a lot less outrage from the pensioners playing bingo that night if you'd left your underwear on." I put the sandwich on a plate and handed it to him.

"Mrs. Cortez hasn't been able to look me in the eye since."

"Yeah, well, she saw more than one of your eyes that night." I grabbed the cloth and cleaned up the island. "I think *I'm* still scarred from that night, never mind poor Mrs. Cortez."

"Poor Mrs. Cortez my ass," he said around a mouthful of food. "The next day, she showed up at my house, told Abuelita what I'd done, and she whipped me with her flip-flop for ten minutes straight. I think I have a scar on my thigh from her attack."

"It worked, though. She beat the urge to flash your ass in public right out of you."

Now, you just do it in private. To your best friend. Ahem.

"I prefer the line that I grew out of the urge." He raised an eyebrow and put down the sandwich to get a bottle of water from my fridge. "It sounds better to prospective girlfriends than 'my crazy Mexican grandmother beat my ass with her shoe.'"

"Prospective girlfriends? You got many of those?"

"No, but it's beside the point."

"It's not, but if it makes you feel better, you believe that." I tossed the dirty cloth in the sink and leaned back against the counter. "You know Abuelita will just tell everyone what she did anyway."

"Yeah, but by that point, I'll have charmed the pants off any prospective girlfriend, and she'll be totally in love with me so it won't matter."

"Clearly, your ego isn't that damaged that much."

"I'm charming as hell. Admit it."

"Luke, you're about as charming as a bout of food poisoning on your wedding day."

"You wound me. How have I kept you around this long?"

"Well," I said, tilting my head to the side. "Do you want me to start with the food part? Or the fact that I know all your secrets?"

He tapped his fingers on the countertop, frowning. "I should probably go for the secrets thing, but it's more likely the food."

I shook my head. "You're insane."

"I know. I just bought you tampons. I must be insane."

"You're talking an awful lot for someone who claims to be hungry."

He answered that with a grin and a huge bite into his sandwich. "So, what's for dinner?"

"Sometimes, I feel like we're an old married couple," I muttered, pushing off the counter and heading for my room. "Lock the door on your way out."

His deep laugh followed me even as I shut my bedroom door behind him.

Best friends. Who needed them?

SIX

LUKE

Food Fixes Everything

I HAULED THE HUGE BOX OF FOOD OUT OF THE trunk of my truck. I had to put it on the floor to shut the trunk and lock the car, then I began the trek up to Aspen's fourth-floor apartment.

Abuelita finally finished making enough food to feed the five hundred, and I wasn't entirely sure Aspen had room in her freezer for all this. She'd even gone so far as to make up taco fillings and freeze them for her.

See? Between Aspen and my grandmother, I had no reason to go grocery shopping. They'd feed me until I either got married or died.

I was likely to die first. Finding a woman as willing to feed me as they were was probably a tall order.

It wasn't that I couldn't cook. I could cook. You didn't

grow up in a Mexican family without being dragged into the kitchen on a semi-regular basis. In fact, I was quite a good cook.

I just didn't *like* to cook.

So I didn't cook. Unless it was absolutely necessary.

It was rarely necessary.

I made it to Aspen's floor and kicked the door a few times in lieu of knocking. I couldn't knock given that I had a restaurant-worthy amount of food in the box I was holding.

The door swung open. Since it was almost eight p.m. and she'd worked the afternoon and early evening shift, I wasn't surprised at all to see Aspen looking the way she did.

No make-up. Hair shoved in a messy twist on top of her head with wisps framing her face. Faded shorts covered with the American flag. An old tank top with sauce from the pizza slice she was holding. And no bra.

Definitely no bra.

"'Sup?" she said with her mouth full of pizza. "What's that?"

"Abuelita kept her promise. It's food."

Her eyes widened, and she leaned right over to look in. "Enchiladas, quesadilla—oh my god, is that taco filling? And homemade nachos?"

"Yes, and they're fucking heavy, so can you move?"

She jumped to the side, clearing the way for me to get in.

I lugged the box inside and breathed a sigh of relief when I was able to put it on the kitchen island. Fuck me, that was heavy. If that didn't prove my love for her as a best friend, I didn't know what would.

Maybe eating dinner at my own place once in a while, but let's not get too crazy.

"You bought pizza?"

She put her slice back down in the box. "Extra-large. It's like I knew you'd be coming," she drawled sarcastically. "Did Abuelita think I was feeding a family of five?"

"No, but she did know that you'd end up feeding me at least forty percent of it."

"Only forty percent?" She quirked a brow and dug through the tubs. "I can freeze some of this stuff, right?"

"Yes. She split the box as she packed it. This side is for freezing," I said, touching the right side. "It's all fillings. They're labeled. Beef and chicken tacos, enchilada, fajita, burrito, and probably more."

"Yummmmm."

"And this side is to eat straight away." I tapped the left side.

She tore off a bite of pizza and looked. "I'll heat up these quesadillas. You want some?"

"You're eating pizza, Asp."

She grabbed two trays of quesadilla and glared at me with her honey-colored eyes. "Are you judging me?"

"A little." My lips twitched.

"Based on the calendar, I have a day and a half left of the worst week of the month. Therefore, I'm running out of time to eat my body weight every six hours. Either shut up, or I'll eat your quesadillas, too."

"Don't play with my food, woman."

"Don't play with me, Luke." She shot me mock daggers and put the quesadillas in the oven to warm through. "So. How was work?"

I pulled a beer from her fridge and took it to the sofa. Her sofa was the comfiest thing I'd ever put my ass on. "Oh, you mean after you sent me running around town for your tampons? Great. I spent two hours being told I was whipped until Julie whipped *them*."

Aspen scoffed, taking her half-eaten slice of pizza and jumping into the armchair. "You can't be whipped. I'm not your girlfriend."

"You think I didn't tell them that?"

"I think they're still hung up on the kiss you claimed happened that never did."

Oh, Jesus. "It was a kiss. Barely, but still one."

"We never kissed." She shook her head, the bun on top of her head wobbling. "You can't add me to that tally."

"I don't have a tally. I'm not fourteen." I paused.

"Besides, is the idea of kissing me really that repulsive?"

You weren't complaining on Saturday...

Aspen sighed, tucking her feet under her ass. Her eyes met mine. "I never said it was repulsive; I merely argued that it never happened. And, for the record, no, I do not find the idea of kissing you repulsive. Just really fucking weird."

"Weird?"

"Well, yeah." She shifted slightly. "That's not the kind of thing you come back from as friends, is it?"

I raised my eyebrows. "Why not?"

"You're starting to sound like you want to kiss me."

"I'd suck a toe before I'd kiss you," I replied. *Lying through my teeth.*

"Okay, there's no need to be mean about it."

"How was that mean?"

"You're right. It wasn't. I'd suck a toe before I'd kiss you, too." She shrugged and licked the pizza sauce off her fingers. "It's just weird, isn't it? Like, we've known each other for twenty years. Can you really imagine us making out?"

Yes.

I can imagine it. Very fucking thoroughly.

Still, I lied, shaking my head. "Hell no."

"Exactly." She pointed at me and got up to check the quesadilla.

I looked away, staring at the TV. Gordon Ramsay's Kitchen Nightmares was on, but the TV was on mute as he rifled through some poor bastard's disgusting freezer.

Talking about kissing her was too much. The memories from Saturday were still seared into my brain, and no matter how much I tried to get rid of them, I couldn't.

Because I knew one thing, no matter how badly the night had ended, kissing her had been a fucking dream.

And I wanted to do it again. Against all rational thought and what I knew was right, I wanted to kiss her again. I wanted to feel her soft lips on mine. My hands in her hair. Her fingers wound into my t-shirt.

Fuck. It was all wrong. I had no damn business sitting here wanting to kiss Aspen. She was my best friend for the love of God—I annoyed her by eating her food, and she annoyed me by asking me to do stupid shit like buy her fucking tampons.

Which I was never doing again.

No amount of food could ever send me back down the psychedelic aisle of ladies' sanitary items.

But still—our relationship had never been based on attraction. Sure, I thought she was beautiful and sexy, but it was more of a casual thought rather than anything I'd ever focused on.

Until now.

Now, I couldn't stop fucking looking at her that way.

Even when she looked like she'd dragged herself through a bush and smeared pizza sauce on her shirt.

She was still beautiful.

And it wasn't just because she was bringing a plate full of my grandmother's quesadilla over to me.

"Here." She handed it to me with a twinkle in her eye. "Because you brought it to me and saved me a trip…and a lesson on keeping a man in my life."

I laughed, taking the plate and cutlery from her. "She did mention that when she gave me the box. She asked me if you were dating a nice young Mexican man yet."

Aspen groaned, tucking one of the wisps of hair behind her ear. "Why is she insistent on my future husband being Mexican?"

"Because she hates the Italians? I don't know. She's Mexican. She thinks everyone should marry Mexican in the hope that one day, we'll be able to take over the world."

"No, that'll be the aliens who take over the world."

"You know how she feels about aliens. They're right up there with the Illuminati."

"I know that, but I only have a very rudimentary understanding of Spanish." Aspen paused, a piece of quesadilla speared onto her fork. "You're the one who gets the rant about conspiracy theorists."

"And that's why I now do my best to not piss you off," I countered. "Because last time, she went on about it for three days."

"She has some very valid arguments."

"You believe in both aliens and the Illuminati."

"Of course I do. There's no way that, in an infinite universe, a race as dumb as humans are the only ones to exist," she said, putting a cushion under her plate and settling it back down. "And as for the Illuminati, well, that's not a conversation you should have out loud."

I rolled my eyes. "You need to spend less time on the internet."

"On the contrary, you need to spend more. You should try Tumblr."

"What's on Tumblr?"

"You're just proving my point, Luke. Go visit Tumblr. It's a gold mine." She grinned and reached for the remote. "How do people still visit restaurants after watching this show? These places are gross."

"That was a one-eighty in conversation I'm not sure how to deal with." I chewed some quesadilla and swallowed. "For the record, I agree with you. These places are gross."

Aspen nodded. "Yet I can't stop watching. It's like a bad drug. A bit like sex. And tequila."

Sex and tequila. Doubly bad when mixed together. I was the fucking authority on that, after all.

"You're telling me," I muttered.

She jerked her head up. "What?"

"I agreed with you," I said quickly. "I was eating."

Her eyes narrowed, but she let it go. We ate in peace after that, with no more mentions of Mexican men or sex or tequila. I was glad of that. I didn't want to think about any of those things in relation to Aspen.

It was going to take a while to move past what had happened, that was for sure. I was just happy it wasn't painfully fucking awkward.

I'm sure it would have been had we both remembered.

My phone buzzed in my pocket with an incoming call. I put the plate on the coffee table in front of me and pulled it out.

It was my grandmother.

"I know who that is," Aspen muttered, hiding a smile behind her hand.

"Hello?" I said, holding the phone to my ear.

A long stream of Spanish exploded into my ear.

"Whoa, calm down," I said. "Speak slowly."

"Does Aspen like the food? Did she meet a nice Mexican boy yet? Why hasn't she called me?" Abuelita's questions came like fireworks on the Fourth of July, one after another.

"You know. Abuelita, I'm not the person to answer that. Let me pass you over."

Aspen was shaking her head with wide eyes before I'd even had a chance to move. "No, no, no!" she mouthed, waving her hands around.

"Yeah, here she is!" I held the phone out with a grin.

Aspen took it, murder in her bright eyes. She jammed the phone against her ear. "Hey, Abuelita. How are you?"

I could hear the buzz from my grandmother's extraordinarily loud voice as I sat back with a grin and ate the rest of my food.

"Yes, the food is great, thank you," Aspen said, turning her back to me. "Quesadilla... Mhmm, he is... Yep... Ah, well, no, I haven't met anyone yet... No, not being picky, just working... Uh-huh... We'll see, maybe... I'll call you as soon as I do... Yes, I promise... Okay, bye!"

She turned on her heel and glared at me.

I held up my hands. "She asked me questions about you. How could I answer those?"

"With your words," she snapped, throwing my phone onto the sofa next to me. "She just told me, in two languages, that I'm twenty-five this weekend, and it's about time I got into a serious relationship, then offered me your cousin, Luis."

I shook my head. "Don't date Luis."

"I didn't intend on dating Luis!"

"You don't need to shout at me."

"She's not even my grandmother! Why is she on my back about getting married? You're two months older than me and you're not getting married either! I didn't sign up for this! My grandparents live in Maine!"

I tried not to laugh. I really fucking did, but I couldn't help myself.

It wasn't every day you had an angry brunette covered in pizza sauce with her nipples poking through her shirt yelling at you about your grandmother trying to marry her off.

Aspen threw a cushion at my head. "You're a dick! Stop laughing at me!"

"I can't." I moved the plate back onto the coffee table and tossed the cushion back at her. "It's so funny. She has an obsession with getting you married. I think she wants you to marry into my family."

"Really? What gave it away?" She stormed over the fridge and pulled out an unopened bottle of wine. "Was it Luis tonight? Or Carlos last year? Or perhaps Juan at Christmas the year before that?"

"I thought you were quitting drinking."

She jammed the corkscrew into the top of the bottle, twisted, and yanked the cork out. "Bite me."

I grabbed my beer and laughed into my hand. "You forgot Javier and Eduardo at my parents' anniversary party."

She slumped forward, groaning as she poured wine into a glass. "Don't. Please don't remind me of that night. It was hell."

"I would have thought Jorge at prom was the worst night."

She held up one hand and drained her glass of wine. "Stop it. I cannot take another set up with one of your cousins. It's not that I have anything against your family, but—"

"It's bad enough dealing with Abuelita as my best friend, never mind being an actual part of the family."

Sighing, she sat back in the chair. "She's insane."

"My entire family is insane. You know that. You would literally be a part of it if she had her way."

"I basically am. I'm an honorary Taylor, even though it annoys her that your mom took your dad's name."

"Every day. Not a week goes by that she doesn't guilt my mom about it, considering all her sisters married Mexican men or kept their surnames." I paused. "Then again, I'm the only one of the grandkids not to be given a Mexican name, so I think my mom rebelled from birth."

Aspen hugged her knee to her chest. "She did. She once told me that she ran shirtless through the middle of town because of a dare. She's where you get your exhibitionist streak from."

That explained so much. "When the hell did she tell you that?"

"At the anniversary party last year, right after she rescued me from your grandmother and Javier."

"Was that before or after my cousins argued over who was going to date you?"

"Before. I seem to remember your aunts clipping them both around the back of the head for being so disrespectful." She tapped a finger against her lips. "I think your Aunt Ana told Eduardo that if he dared fight over a woman like a stray dog over a raw piece of steak again, she'd beat respect into his ass."

I nodded slowly. "I think she did that later that night when he hit on Blaire. Except Blaire punched him."

"Probably," Aspen agreed. "Blaire is quite violent if you piss her off."

"No kidding," I replied. "I do actually have a scar on my foot from where she stomped on it when she thought I was hitting on her sister."

She rolled her eyes and met my gaze. "You were hitting on her sister."

"I touched her tit by accident. She moved, I moved, the flirting went wrong…" I shrugged. "I'm not exactly James Bond."

"I know that. Daniel Craig is way hotter than you for an old guy."

"Are you seriously telling me that some blonde, British dude who's about fifty years old is hotter than me? Half Mexican, dark, mysterious—"

She almost spilled her wine as she snorted.

"Mysterious? You're mysterious? You're not Superman!"

"I'm totally mysterious. I'm the tall, dark, handsome guy women fawn over in romance books. I have the hair, the eyes, the abs…"

"Complete with a crazy ass grandma who'd scare any half-sensible woman off," she continued, speaking slowly like I was stupid. "Pretty sure any future wife of yours will have to be a superhero in her own right."

"You can tutor them in managing my family." I grinned.

"Uh… No. Nobody taught me. If I've lasted twenty years, so can some other poor asshole."

"I resent you referring to my future wife as an asshole."

"Let's face it." She rested on the arm of the sofa, twirling her wine glass, and raised her eyebrows. "Anyone who puts up with you has to be a little bit of an asshole."

"Are you calling me an asshole?"

"You need a special touch. A little *je ne sais quoi.*"

"A little something you don't know?"

"It sounds better in French." She laughed, covering the lower part of her face with her hand.

She was fucking pretty when she laughed. Her eyes lit up, and she had this stupid little dimple on her right cheek I'd never really cared about until now.

No wonder Eduardo and Javier had fought over her. I might have, had I been the given the option.

"I'm just saying that you're a little bit of a handful. With your family and the food and your proclivity for getting naked…" Her eyes sparkled. "You need a wife with a firm touch."

"I need a wife who can cook and withhold tequila."

"Damn it, that puts me out of the running."

"You can cook."

"Yeah, but I'm bad at withholding alcohol." She held up her glass to punctuate her point. "But, for the record, I can't wait for you to get married. I might get to keep food in my fridge longer than twenty-four hours."

"Like I told you, stop going to the grocery store."

"I can't. If I stop going, you'll eat what little food I do have anyway." She tilted the glass in my direction. "Don't you have to be up early for work tomorrow instead of ruining my nice quiet night?"

I ran my hand through my hair. "I do, but I'm pretty invested in this restaurant now."

"You haven't watched half of it."

"So rewind it so I can. It's not my fault you keep talking at me."

Aspen sighed and got up, grabbing the controller. She paused for a second, then doubled back to the kitchen. She grabbed the bottle of wine from the fridge and brought it over to the sofa. "Here. It's recorded."

I took the remote. "You record this?"

"Every night. You got a problem with that?"

"No," I said, hitting the button to start it from the beginning. "But you're not exactly giving me a reason to stop eating your food."

She side-eyed me and snatched the remote, but her lips were twitching to one side. "Like that could ever happen."

I nudged her with my elbow and winked. "True story."

SEVEN

ASPEN

I Didn't Sign Up For This

I DIDN'T UNDERSTAND HOW THIS WAS happening.

It felt like just thirty seconds ago I wished Luke goodnight in the living room with the sofa as his makeshift bed.

Now, here he was.

In my bed.

With his face between my legs.

Yup. I was lying on my back, legs wide open, with my best friend's face buried between them.

And I was enjoying it.

Holy shit, I was. I didn't have time to think about how the hell we'd ended up in this situation, because all I could focus on was how he moved his tongue.

He flicked it over my clit, teasing me as my muscles twitched. My back arched, and he gripped my hips with his large hands, holding me in place against him. Pleasure darted through me, and my fingers wound themselves in the sheet beneath me.

Holy hell.

He toyed with me with his tongue—bringing me to the brink of orgasm before he kissed the inside of my thigh. I moaned as he left me there, hovering on the edge, staring into the oblivion with the sick knowledge that I'd have to wait for the release I so desperately wanted.

Luke kissed his way up my body, his naked one covering mine. His hands explored my curves, leaving no inch of me uncovered. He circled his lips over my nipples, flicking his tongue over them the way he just had my clit.

I ran my hands up his back and into his thick, dark hair. His lips found mine with a breathy exhale. Our bodies melded together like they were supposed to, and desire burst through my veins with a red-hot flush that made goosebumps dance across my skin.

I wanted him. I wanted to feel him for real. I knew that night was a bad fluke and that this would be better.

I needed the closure that would come from this.

I needed this so we could move on with our friendship.

We kissed deeper, our tongues battling. The taste of me lingered on his lips, but I kept kissing him, lifting my legs and winding them around his waist. It was a silent plea for him to move inside me.

His cock was hard and pressed against my pussy, brushing just against my clit in the most tempting way.

"Luke," I whispered against his lips. "Please."

He laughed softly, cupping the back of my neck. "Are you actually begging me?"

"Yes," I moaned, trying to reach down between us to grab his cock.

He beat me to it. He adjusted his hips so he could position himself correctly and sat up, looking down between us as the tip of his cock brushed against my clit.

I tilted my hips up to make it easier for him. Slowly, he guided his cock to the opening of my pussy and gently pushed himself into me. Inch by inch, my wet pussy clenched around him, and I drew in a deep breath.

He paused when he was inside me, his eyes firmly fixated on mine. Leaning forward, he cupped the side of my face and kissed me again.

Then he moved.

Slowly.

In and out, a rhythmic motion that felt so damn good I could barely stand it.

My fingers slipped back into his hair, curling around his thick locks. Our bodies moved together like magic. Pleasure came at me in waves that I couldn't control.

I just wanted the release.

I wanted to come, to finally feel what it was like to—

The jolt was sharp and unwelcome.

I blinked, sleep making my lashes feel thick and heavy. My room was pitch black, and not only was I alone, but the covers felt like they weighed about a hundred pounds.

And they were hot.

Just like I was.

I peeled the covers off my sweaty body and rolled to the side. I was sticking to the sheet, so I had no choice but to haul my sleepy ass out of bed and crack open my bedroom window.

I pulled open one curtain, opened the window, and leaned against the windowsill.

What the hell had just happened?

Had I just had a very real, very dirty dream about Luke? Who was sleeping on my sofa in the next room?

Shit, I had.

And I'd liked it. My clit was throbbing, and my heart was racing. I swear I was seconds from actually having an orgasm in my sleep.

Oh god, I'd sleep-fucked Luke.

And it'd been more satisfying than the real time we'd done it.

Why'd I have to wake up? It was going well until that point. Really, really well, actually. That was why I was in a hot little tizzy over it.

The gentle breeze that crept through my cracked window was more warm and sticky than it was soothing, so I shut the door and moved to sit back on my bed, leaving the curtain open. A faint orange glow from the lights on the street below my building shone through the window, illuminating the corner of my room with a gauzy haze.

I ran my fingers through my hair and looked out of the window. I couldn't see much thanks to the fog that had rolled in off the beach, but looking at nothing was better than thinking about what I'd just dreamed about.

Jesus, what if I'd made noises? Had I? What if Luke had heard? He was sleeping on my couch after all. How the hell was I supposed to face him in a few hours knowing what I'd been dreaming about?

How was I supposed to go back to sleep? What if my mind took me back to that dream? I couldn't see out the end of that. There was no way—did you moan if you came in your sleep? Was it loud like normal?

I didn't know. I'd never had a sleep-orgasm before. I'd never had a dirty dream in my life.

Until tonight.

Was there an etiquette for this? Did I go back to sleep? Did I lie and stare at the ceiling for hours? Did I go on Buzzfeed and find out what kind of cheese I was?

I sighed, cupping the back of my neck and linking my

fingers.

This was a disaster. What if I accidentally mentioned this to him?

Why did we have to have bad sex? If we'd never done that, if we'd just passed out, fully clothed, on my bed, the way we always did, none of this would have happened.

Why that night? Why now? Why, why, why?

I stood up and quietly made my way to my door. Thankfully, it wasn't creaky, and I was able to open it without making any noise. I paused, peering over at the sofa to make sure Luke was asleep.

He was. He was lying flat on it, one arm slung over the top of his head, and his feet were dangling off the end of the end of it. His clothes were in a pile on the floor next to the sofa, and the blanket I'd tossed his way before bed was only covering his legs.

I tried not to look at his sculpted, toned stomach as I tiptoed my way to the kitchen to get a bottle of water. The fridge squeaked as I opened the door, and the light from the inside cast a dim glow over the living room.

I winced, pulling the bottle from the door and closing the fridge quickly.

"Aspen?"

I stepped back, hugging the water as Luke sat up on the sofa, using the back of it to haul himself up. "Sorry," I said quietly. "I needed some water. I tried not to wake you."

He waved his hand. "You all right?"

"Yeah—uh, bad dream."

He frowned, pushing his fingers through his hair. "You get chased by a giant penguin again?"

I bit the inside of my cheek so he didn't catch me laughing. "Yep. Razor-teeth and everything this time."

Luke moved so he was sitting up fully. "Can you grab me a bottle of water?"

"Sure." I pulled a bottle from the fridge and took it over to him, then perched on the arm of the sofa he'd just moved his feet from.

"Thanks. You feel okay?"

I nodded and shook my water, deliberately not making eye contact with him. I didn't think I could do that right now. "Sorry I woke you."

He took a long drink from the bottle and waved me away again. "Don't worry about it. Your sofa isn't exactly the most comfortable thing in the world."

"Sorry. You wanna swap?"

"I'm not making you sleep on your sofa. What time is it?"

"Like two or something." I yawned, covering my mouth with my hand. "I don't mind."

"No, it's good. I'll come sleep with you."

My eyes widened. No, no, no. That wasn't good. I couldn't have him in my bed. No way. There was no chance

I'd get back to sleep if we were in the same bed.

He quirked a brow at me. "What's that look for? You want me to put pants on?"

"Are you naked under there?"

"No. I have my boxers on." He paused. "You sure you're all right, Asp? It's not like we've never shared a bed. You're acting weird."

Crap.

"Um, no, it's fine. Sorry. I'm still half-asleep. Come on." I got up and hurried into my room before I had to see him practically naked.

By the time he joined me, I'd closed my curtains and climbed into bed with my back to the door—and him.

The click of my door shutting told me he was in the room, and the clunk of his water bottle on the nightstand preceded the huge dip in the mattress as he joined me in bed.

I wriggled over a little further, tucking the sheets around me as much as I could.

"You're moving like I've got a deadly disease," Luke muttered, making the mattress bounce as he got comfortable.

"You snore," I muttered right back. "And you'll end up taking up most of the bed anyway, so I'm saving myself the pain of having your elbow in my spine in an hour."

He chuckled. "If you say so. You're the wriggler."

"Whatever."

"You're still acting weird." He reached over and poked me.

"It's two in the morning, and there's a strange man in my bed. Shut up."

"I'm not a stranger."

"I didn't say you were a stranger. I said you were a strange man, and you are." I tugged the covers in a little tighter to me. "Now shut up and go to sleep."

He laughed quietly, rolling onto his back. "Night, Aspen."

"Night."

That was the last time we binged Gordon Ramsay's Kitchen Nightmares.

THANKFULLY, ANY NAUGHTY DREAMS STAYED well away from my mind for the remainder of the night.

I'd never been so happy about anything. The last thing I wanted was to have to explain to Luke why the hell I was having sleep orgasms while in bed next to him.

I also didn't want to have to admit that I hadn't had a bad dream, either.

Overgrown penguins aside, he was up and stealing my

hot water before I'd even opened my eyes. I rubbed my face, removing the sleep from my eyes, and got up to the tune of my shower battering against the tiles.

It wasn't the best alarm in the world, considering I really wasn't a morning person. I worked at a bar for a reason. The earliest I ever had to go into work was two p.m., and that was often the time I clocked off.

I liked it that way.

If I'd been born in October instead of July, I was pretty sure I'd have been born a witch.

I grabbed some clean clothes and quickly changed, almost falling over in my race to get my clean panties on. Luckily for me, I managed it, and I was just pulling my 'what the cluck' shirt over my head when the water stopped running in the bathroom.

The bedroom door creaked open until I could see one of his eyes peeking through. "Are you awake? I left my clothes in here."

Laughing, I nodded. "I'm awake, and I'm changed. Don't worry."

"Wouldn't be the first time I saw you naked," he muttered.

I blushed. "Being nine in the swimming pool doesn't count."

He rolled his eyes and walked into the room.

I could do nothing but burst into laughter.

Luke stopped, then looked down at the pink towel with white flowers all over it that was wrapped around his waist. He shrugged. "I'm comfortable with my masculinity. Laugh all you like—I look good in any kind of towel."

"Wow, okay, Mr. Ego. Calm down. You do need to leave this apartment to go to work, and you keep on like that, you won't be able to get your head through this door," I said, injecting a final burst of sarcasm into the last few words as I left him and his stupidly hot body in my bedroom and my girly towel.

Seriously. I'd laughed at the towel, but there was no laughing at—

The man who'd followed me into the kitchen.

"Sorry," he said, reaching around me to get the steaming mug of coffee from the machine. "I made it before I got in the shower."

"And here I thought you'd made me a coffee to say thank you for not complaining that you had your elbow in my back for an hour last night." It wasn't the only thing I think he'd had near my back, but I wasn't going to bring that up right now.

Plus, I wasn't sure. It could have been his finger. That was a long shot, but I was going with finger.

"You want it?" His dark hair flopped down over his forehead, dripping water down his face. "You can have it. I'll make another."

I blinked at him. "Uh, sure."

"You don't want it?"

"I want it." I slid the cup toward me before he could decide I didn't. "I just wasn't expecting you to give it to me."

"Well, you're right—I did sleep with my elbow in your back for a while last night until you smacked me in the face with your pillow." He shrugged one shoulder. "Giving you my coffee is the least I can do for poking you half the night."

Oh man, he poked me a hell of a lot more last night than he knew.

I dipped my head before he could see me blush. The memory of that dream, combined with him standing in front of me with his tanned body still wet, with water droplets dancing down across his abs and disappearing into the…pink towel.

Wow. The pink towel really ruined that fantasy, didn't it?

I shook my head as I grabbed the milk from the fridge for my coffee. Fantasy ruiner or not, all you had to do was look above the pink towel to know exactly why him half-naked plus the memory of the dream was dangerous.

Every day, every time I looked at Luke, it seemed like I had a reason to look at him in a new light, and looking at him as anything other than my best friend felt weird.

Not wrong, but weird.

I didn't want to blush at the sight of water droplets trickling between his abs. I didn't want to find the veins on his forearms sexy. I didn't want to flick his hair back from his forehead and lick the water from his lips.

But I did.

And I was highly uncomfortable with this new turn of events.

You weren't supposed to lust after your best friend.

You weren't supposed to imagine licking water drops off him or hugging him just so you could whip off his towel. You weren't supposed to blush at the sight of him wet and in a towel.

Nope.

None of this was supposed to be happening.

And here I'd thought that our drunken night hadn't changed anything.

In reality, it'd changed just about fucking everything.

And I hadn't signed up for all these changes.

Not a single damn one.

EIGHT
ASPEN

Stop The World, I Want To Get Off

"SO, YOU SLEPT TOGETHER RIGHT AFTER YOU had a dirty dream about it?" Blaire leaned over the bar, resting on her forearms. "Dude, what's wrong with you?"

"We didn't sleep together," I hissed, glancing around the bar to see if I was needed. I wasn't. Phew. "I had a dirty dream, went to get water, and I woke him up, so he slept in my bed instead."

"So you slept together. Technically." Her eyes glittered.

"Fine. Technically." I pressed my hands against my cheeks. "What do I do, Blaire? What am I supposed to do now?"

She held up her hands briefly before cradling her wine glass. "I've told you what I think you should do, but you won't listen to me."

I sighed. "I can't tell him. It's not even awkward. Like, aside from these stupid thoughts I'm having, nothing has changed. We're still the same as we've always been."

"You're having dirty dreams about your best friend eating your pussy. How is that the same?"

"I said aside from those stupid thoughts," I said through gritted teeth. "And say it a little louder, I don't think those college frat boys in the corner heard you."

Blaire looked over her shoulder. All four of them were looking over at us, and they looked a little too interested in what we were saying.

"Sorry," she said quieter. "I just—I don't get you two."

"Neither do I," I muttered, sliding down the bar to take an empty glass that had just been put on it. "Maybe it's just something I need to work through. You know, get it out of my system with a few more dreams."

"And a handy vibrating friend?"

"If all else fails, yes." I nodded resolutely. "If that's my only option, that's what I'll have to do."

"You say that like you're making a great sacrifice for all of womankind."

"I'm sacrificing my morals."

"Your morals? What? To never masturbate over your best friend?"

I paused. Actually, yes. Then again, I'd never been in a situation where I'd been forced to consider masturbating over Luke Taylor.

"Can I get a beer?" One of the frat boys asked, standing a few feet away from Blaire.

Thank heavens for small mercies.

"Sure. Can I see your ID?" I held my hand out for it.

"I already showed it."

"To the girl who was here before. Not to me." I wiggled my fingers in a 'gimme' motion.

He grumbled something under his breath but handed me his license. I took it, glanced at the date, and handed it back with a smile, then grabbed a bottle of what he'd been drinking before from the fridge.

"So, I heard what your friend was saying…"

"Finishing that sentence is the fastest way to get your ass kicked out of my bar," I replied, popping the cap on the beer and handing it to him.

"Right." He smiled sheepishly and handed me a five.

I took it and returned his change to him, watching as he went over to his little buddies and leaned in to speak to them.

"I love it when you shoot assholes down," Blaire said, finishing her wine. "It's almost as fun as tearing Justin a new asshole."

"No. Nothing is as fun as tearing Justin a new asshole." I shook my head and grabbed a bottle of wine from the fridge. I emptied it into her glass and added it to her tab.

"So, back to Luke." She grinned.

"Let's not get back to Luke." I tossed the bottle in the tub by my feet and leaned on the bar. "What the hell do I do?"

"I don't know. I've told you, you won't listen to me, and now I'm tired of your crap."

"I love you, too."

"I know. I'm just keeping it real. You need someone to keep you grounded." She sipped her wine again, smiling behind the glass. "I think you need to go on a date. Or pull someone on your birthday. A one-night stand is what you need to get him out of your system. Maybe you don't need to fuck Luke—maybe you just need to fuck somebody."

Laughter came from the college guys in the corner.

Maybe this wasn't the perfect place to have this conversation after all.

Whatever.

"I don't think so," I said slowly. "You know how I feel about one-night stands."

"And you're wrong. They're delightful," Blaire replied.

"You have a boyfriend."

"How do you think I met Tom?"

I laughed, burying my face in my hands. "Okay, fine, but that's not me. I'm not a hump and dump girl."

"Asp, you just fucked your best friend. In real life and in your dreams. Not many people get to say that."

"Many people are lucky they don't get to say that." I slammed a glass on the bar and filled it with Pepsi. "I'd like to be one of those lucky little fuckers."

"Then you should have kept it in your pants."

"You're right. I should have." There was no denying that. This whole situation wouldn't exist if I'd kept it in my pants.

Although, Luke had fifty percent of the blame here. He should have kept it in his pants, too.

I sipped my Pepsi and sighed. "I'm not going out for my birthday. After last weekend, I think I need to stay locked in my apartment, a million miles away from tequila or any other form of alcohol."

"We're going out," Blaire said, shaking her head. "There's no way you can stay in. It's your birthday."

"I know, but I don't want to. I cannot think of anything worse than going out and doing a repeat of last week."

"It's really quite simple not to."

"Yeah, yeah, keep my pants on. Whatever." I rolled my eyes and put a slice of lemon in my Pepsi. "Look, I'm not going out. I know exactly what will happen. I'll get talked into tequila—who, at this point, is right on my shit list— and then I'll end up telling Luke what happened, and there'll be no more ignoring it."

"Okay, but," Blaire said, holding up one finger with a Barbie-pink nail. "You're not really ignoring it. We keep talking about it. You're dreaming about it. You're even starting to be weird around Luke now. Getting drunk and telling him might not be the worst idea."

"Really? You don't think that it's the worst thing I could do? Jesus, do you want to watch me crash and burn?" I waved goodbye to a customer and took the tip they'd left on the bar, then turned to put it in the jar.

"As fun as that might be, no." She grinned. "But if it happens, it happens."

"It won't happen. I'm not drinking."

"What won't happen?" Luke's deep tones cut into the conversation.

I jumped, turning around and almost slipping on a lime wedge on the floor. Ignoring his chuckle that was punctuated by Blaire's snort, I picked it up and tossed it into the little trash can.

"You scared the hell out of me," I said, finally giving him some attention.

He grinned, his damp hair a hot mess on top of his head. "Sorry. I thought you saw me come in."

"Nah, she's not with it." Blaire sipped her wine. "As evidenced by her claim that she's not going out for her birthday."

Luke nodded as I grabbed his favorite beer from the fridge. "I heard that, too. What excuse is she giving you?"

"She wants to remember a Saturday night for once,"

Blaire said without missing a beat. "Since she's still a little fuzzy on a few things last weekend."

"Not a bad plan," he replied, taking the beer with a smile. "I can't remember much either."

"You could just drink in moderation." Blaire turned to me.

I snorted. "With you around? Yeah, whatever. Like that'll happen."

"Are you calling me an enabler?"

"Yes," Luke and I both answered at the same time.

She pressed her hand to her chest, the bright pink of her nails a stark contrast against her black blouse. "I cannot believe you would say that. When have I ever enabled you?"

"Last weekend," Luke answered.

"Your birthday," I added.

"New Years was rough," Luke continued.

I nodded. "I still don't think I can do Halloween this year after last year."

He grimaced. "And that doesn't even count your birthday from last year."

"All right, all right." Blaire held up her hands. "But you two are entirely responsible for your actions. You don't need to give in when I push shots on you."

"Or you could not push the shots," Luke replied.

"Or you could just be responsible for your actions," she repeated, this time a lot slower. The bitch even made sure to look me right in the eye.

I resisted the urge to flip her off—but only just, and that was because a customer needed me. If we'd been anywhere else, I'd have done it. Or punched her.

Probably punched her.

When I was done serving, I rejoined my best friends at their end of the bar and interrupted their hushed conversation.

"What are you talking about?" I grabbed my Pepsi from the shelf under the bar and finished it.

"How you'll get drunk on your birthday," Blaire replied. "You know you will. Put a tray of tequila in front of you, and you can't help but drink it."

"I swear to God, I'm not going to."

The familiar deep chuckle of my boss, Declan, filled the air. His large hand brushed across my shoulder as he stepped out from the back and joined me behind the bar. "Sure you won't, Aspen. We all believe you."

I rolled my eyes, ignoring my Greek-god-looking boss... If you ignored the slightly round belly. "I swear to God. No. It's not happening."

"You said that on Saturday, and I had to pile all three of your asses into my brother's cab to get y'all home." Declan filled a glass with lemonade for him and scanned all three of us. "This is why y'all are forbidden from drinkin' anywhere but here."

Blaire batted her eyelashes. "And here I was thinkin' it's 'cause you liked us."

"It helps that I get your money, too." He winked and picked up his glass. "Y'all will come in here on Friday night for Aspen's birthday, drink all my tequila, and I'll pile your butts into that same cab to take y'all home."

Seriously. All he needed was cowboy boots and plant or something in his mouth to chew like a regular farmer with all the accent he put on when he was trying to talk to us like he was our dad.

"And don't bat your lashes at me like that, Blaire Carpenter. I remember you flashin' your boobs like they were an S.O.S signal on your twenty-first birthday."

I dipped my head, trying to hide my laugh.

The more our respective birthdays and drunken antics were brought up, the more I realized we really had to grow up a little.

Maybe.

I mean, growing up was overrated. I already had to pay rent and bills and taxes—I needed to get my kicks where I could get them.

Sometimes, that was lying on the sofa, half-naked, holding my boobs like they were a comfort blanket.

Other times, it was getting dressed up, drinking my body weight in tequila, and making bad decisions.

Look. I couldn't be responsible all the time.

I wasn't my mother.

I was an almost twenty-five-year-old borderline hot mess with an attraction to tequila and a habit of making terribly bad choices.

I was, shock horror, human.

And apparently, given my questionable choice of best friend, that wasn't changing any time soon.

"So. Should I book y'all out the back room for your birthday?" Declan said, ringing up an order from a customer.

"Yes," Blaire said before I could say anything. "And put a sofa and blanket in it in case Grandma here needs to take a nap."

"I'm younger than you, you little shit," I replied, pointing at her before I turned to Declan. "Yes, book it. Whatever. Control the amount of tequila put into me, okay?"

He chuckled, scratching the back of his neck. "Aspen, honey, you're an adult."

"And I pay my rent on time every month and haven't had my cable cut in two years," I shot back. "Help me out a little here."

He held his hands up. "If that's your greatest achievement, I can't help you."

I rolled my eyes and took Luke's empty beer bottle. "You having another?"

"Better not. I have to see old Eddie tomorrow, and if he thinks I'm unfit to do the job, Vicky might just kill me."

Blaire snorted. "Your boss would kill a worm if it was in her path."

"Yeah, and I wonder what traits she passed to her niece," I drawled, giving her a hard, long look.

"The women in my family are bitches. So sue me. We're only bitches because we say it as it is." She returned my pointed look with one of her own and finished the rest of her wine. Slapping a twenty down on the bar, she said, "Keep the change, Grandma. I'm off to see a man about some penis."

Luke dropped his chin to his chest, doing his best to hide his laughter, but Declan stared at her like she'd just dropped the 'C' word in front of a group of tweens.

"I didn't need to hear that," he said sternly. "And neither did anyone else."

Blaire winked, grinned, and left the bar.

"That girl," Declan muttered, shaking his head and heading for the back room.

"Is insane," Luke continued, grinning at me. "You okay to get home tonight?"

"I think I know my way from here to my apartment block." My lips twitched to the side. "But thank you for checking."

He stood, saluting me with two fingers and a lopsided

grin. "You've gotten lost before."

"I'm not ten tequila shots in tonight," I reminded him, catching the eye of a customer at the end of the bar. "I can remember."

He muttered something under his breath that I couldn't quite catch, but I didn't have time to question it thanks to the customer.

Luke met my eyes one more time, throwing up a hand in goodbye, and left.

And I got back to work, definitely not thinking that his lopsided smile was kind of cute.

NINE

LUKE

Boners Galore

AT LEAST SHE REMEMBERED SOMETHING.

Not that I wanted her to remember. No. The more I thought about it, the happier I was that she didn't remember what we'd done.

Our friendship hadn't changed. It was a little awkward, but I was ninety-nine percent sure that was me being a little more reserved and just Aspen being… Aspen.

She had a propensity for putting her foot in her mouth, and while she'd been well-behaved the last few days, that never lasted long once Blaire put tequila in front of her.

That said, I gave it until approximately ten-thirty on Saturday night before she said something to someone.

With any luck, Saturday night would reset the

whole situation I found myself in. We'd all drink, someone would do something stupid—but not two-people kinda stupid—and then the Fourth could all be forgotten.

That was what I wanted.

Judging by the state of my cock when I'd woken up this morning, it wasn't listening to me.

No. Apparently, having bad sex with Aspen had just made me want to have good sex with her. Which meant early-morning boners that were especially inconvenient when I'd been sleeping next to her.

I'd never been so fucking glad to get in the shower before she'd woken up.

It'd taken five minutes of uncomfortably cold water to get rid of that stupid-ass boner that'd plagued me.

And I was fucking dreading going to sleep tonight.

Waking up with a boner was part of being male. I accepted that. Hell, I'd accepted it ever since I was thirteen and got one in the middle of math class. If I thought algebra would help get rid of it in this situation, I'd haul ass to the local high school to sit through a class.

Waking up with a boner over my best friend was a new one. Every time I looked at her, I saw her in a different light. I saw her hair disheveled and her eyes sparkling. I saw her lips swollen and her chin a little red from the stubble on my jaw.

Then, I saw her fake-it face, and I had to wonder how close it was to her real sex face.

I'd put money on it being pretty close.

Because let's face it. Women were master orgasm fakers. If we'd had sex that had lasted longer than two minutes, I probably wouldn't have even been able to tell.

No woman could orgasm in two minutes.

No matter what porn told you.

Really, porn just gave men everywhere an unrealistic expectation of how easy it was to make a woman orgasm.

And female bodies, but that was a point for another day.

I was in hell. Or I was as close to it as I fucking could be.

I was ready to ship to Bermuda and never see her face again. That was the easiest situation here.

The worst part? I didn't even have anyone to talk to about this. Blaire was definitely off the table—no matter that she could actually keep a secret, she'd never keep this from Aspen, and I'd never ask her to.

If I told Tom, he'd tell Blaire, who'd tell Aspen.

This was the problem with small towns. There was always a trail.

With a sigh, I pushed open the door to my parents'

house.

"Luke? Is that you?" Dad appeared in the hallway. "Thank God. You have to help me, son. They're planning your cousin's quinceanera, and they want my help."

I frowned, closing the door behind me. "Elena's? But she's not fifteen until next November."

"Exactly." He pinched the top of his nose and shook his head, eyes briefly closed. "Your grandmother is pitching a fit that there isn't a venue booked yet."

"She did this with Maria and Teresa. She knows we can't book the venue until a year out."

"Will you tell her that?"

"Hell no." I snorted and walked into the kitchen. "She's Mom's mom. She can do that."

"Madre!" Mom shouted from the living room, followed by a long string of Spanish.

I paused at the fridge, looking back at Dad. "Has she been shouting in Spanish long?"

"Yes, but they started off singing Despacito. The 'proper' version, not that one with the little blond boy in it."

"Justin Bieber."

"I don't care what his name is, son. I was just happy when they let the cats back out into the alley." He bustled over to the coffee machine. "Then, your aunt called and mentioned about Elena's birthday and wanting to take her away for the weekend—"

I winced.

"—Which set off your grandmother."

On cue, Abuelita's thick accent broke through the walls as she let off a huge stream of Spanish.

I tilted my head to the side. "Did she just tell Mom that she isn't too old for la chancla?"

Dad snorted. "That's the third time she's threatened it, and her flip-flop has stayed firmly in the closet."

"That's some shit," I replied. "I never even used to get threatened. Just hit."

"Yes, but your mother hasn't been mooning the old people in the bingo hall."

"No, she just skinny-dipped on her twenty-first birthday and never told Abuelita," I muttered.

Dad laughed. "That was a fun night."

"So was my birthday."

He nodded his head. "Point taken. But your mistake was letting your grandmother find out about it."

"Letting her find out about anything is a mistake." I sat on the wooden stool at the island and paused as she and Mom went back and forth in the living room. "How can one party be so much hard work for them? And why is Mom having this argument and not Aunt Val?"

"Valentina is too busy with her new boyfriend, which

also set off your grandmother," Dad said dryly. "In fact, I don't think your mom spoke to her except to answer the phone."

Ah, yes, good old Aunt Val who divorced her nice, Mexican husband and was now dating a younger Canadian man.

We didn't know what pissed Abuelita off more. The fact she'd gotten divorced, or that she was dating a Canadian. After all, the woman hated just about anyone who wasn't one: Mexican, or two: my dad, Aspen, or Blaire.

Even then, I think she tolerated my dad most days. He tolerated her every day, though, so it worked out.

"Luke!" Abuelita chose then to make her grand entrance, sweeping me into a huge bear hug that would have crushed me had I been a few pounds less of muscle.

Abuelita was everything anyone could imagine an old Mexican lady to be—except her clothing style. That was decidedly gypsy.

Not that we'd ever say it out loud.

Standing at a tiny five-foot-tall, she had dark hair that was permanently pulled back into a twist at the nape of her neck. She almost always wore a bandana over her head like she lived in the desert, and her round, wrinkled face was never to be seen without her favorite mascara lining her tiny, dark eyes, and light pink lipstick on thin lips.

Her green skirt swished around her legs as she let go of me. Speaking in Spanish, as always, she said, "Where is Aspen?"

I sighed and replied in English. "At work, Abuelita."

"Why don't you bring her to see me?"

"She's at work. She can't just stop to come and see you."

"No. You no bring her. You ring her. I cook for her." She'd made a rare switch to English, accompanying it with a jab to her chest. "She like my food."

Every word came out like there was a full stop between them.

She. Like. My. Food.

That only meant one thing.

She was annoyed at me.

That wasn't exactly a rare occurrence.

Unlike my mother who switched to Spanish when she was angry, Abuelita switched to English, like the thought she had to put into each broken sentence made her sound angrier.

If I didn't know the damage she could do with a flip-flop, I'd laugh.

"You're absolutely right," I said, placating her. "I'll tell her to stop by when I see her next. She told me to tell you thank you for the food, by the way."

"You call. Now." She pointed at me, the bracelets on her wrist jingling when she wiggled her arm.

Jesus. Sometimes managing her was like managing a basket of kittens in the rain.

"I can't call her, Abuelita. She's at work. The bar was getting busy when I left."

"You call!"

"For the love of—Maria!" Dad's spoon clattered against the counter. "The girl is at work. She can't drop everything on your whim."

Abuelita turned to him, her tiny eyes getting even smaller as she narrowed them. If it was possible, her already-thin lips spread even thinner, and she leaned forward just a tiny amount.

I knew that look.

I'd last seen it right before she'd whipped her flip-flop around the back of my head.

Three times.

"La chancla," she warned him menacingly, waving an imaginary shoe in the air.

She held her hard gaze on him for one more second, then opened the nearest cupboard. A bag of chips landed on the island in front of me, and in silence, she went to the fridge, pulled out a jar, and emptied it into a small glass bowl, then gave me that too.

Salsa.

"You eat. You skinny," she said firmly, looking at me like I'd be the next on the end of her la chancla threat if I didn't agree.

I was smart.

I nodded and opened the chips.

"Jesus, Maria! He's one-hundred-ninety pounds of solid muscle! I've seen gym rats skinnier than him!" Dad threw his hands up in the air.

Abuelita turned on him, and I could have sworn she was going for his mug. Instead, she waved her hand through the air. "Pah!" was the punctuation for her movement, and she snapped a few words in Spanish as she left.

I dipped a chip in salsa and shoved it in my mouth.

"What did she just call me?" Dad asked.

"Stupid American bastard," I replied without batting an eyelid.

Dad put his coffee on the island and leaned in the direction of the door. "Stupid ancient hag!"

"She'll get la chancla," I warned him around another mouthful of chips and salsa.

"Yeah, well, if she weren't such a damn good cook I'd have la chancla'd her obnoxious ass to the grave ten years ago," he muttered, dipping his chip into the bowl of salsa.

"On the bright side, that'll be Mom in twenty years."

"You call that a bright side?" Dad stuck his hand in the

chip packet. "I call that damn bad luck."

He probably wasn't wrong.

"AT LEAST SHE DIDN'T ASK IF I WAS DATING anyone yet," Aspen said, looking at the menu like she didn't know what she was going to get.

Blaire snorted. "Yeah, but now you've agreed to go see her tomorrow on your birthday, and she's going to drill you then."

"Oh no." She looked at me, eyes wide. "Get me out of it."

"Nope." I laughed and grabbed my Coke. "You agreed. You know what she's like. Dad called me this morning and said she's still ignoring him, but every time she sees him, she's waving her hand with an imaginary shoe."

Blaire shuddered. "That's the thing of nightmares."

"She's five-foot-tall."

"The last time I watched her get that thing out to you, you shrieked," she said flatly. "She's terrifying, and you know it."

"I didn't shriek," I said. "I swore."

"You shrieked," Aspen said, grinning. "It was the best day of my life."

"I'm glad my pain brings you amusement."

She opened her mouth to speak, but Blaire's phone rang. She pulled it out of her luggage-sized purse. "Ugh, it's my boss. I'll be right back."

She left the table, and I stared at her leaving.

"How the hell does she find anything in that purse?" I asked, turning my attention back to Aspen.

She shrugged. "She's like Hermione without the magic."

"Yeah, well, if she's got a fucking tent in there, I want some new friends."

"If she's got a tent in there, she needs a therapist." She put the menu down. "Should we wait for Blaire to get back before we order?"

"We can, but we both know that when her boss calls, it's because she needs to leave because the printer stopped working or something."

Aspen laughed.

Blaire's boss was an aging lawyer who couldn't understand the majority of modern-day technology. At this point, he was little more than the guy who ran the law firm while the younger lawyers who could use a laptop without electrocuting themselves did the work. He was also a stickler for not asking for help unless your name was Blaire.

"Do you remember that time we were having dinner with her and Tom when they'd just started dating and he called her? We'd finished eating an hour before—"

The memory made me laugh. "And you and her were well into your second bottle of wine, and he needed an urgent email sent to one of the other lawyers. Didn't she assure him she'd do it, then when he called the next day made up some excuse?"

Aspen nodded, pulling her Coke toward her. "She said her email had been playing up and the message was stuck in her outbox. Not that he knew what the outbox was."

"That probably worked in her favor."

"That and one of the other secretaries promised not to tell him she'd been out drinking if she introduced her to you."

A chill ran down my spine, making me shudder. "What was her name again?"

She shrugged. "How would I know? You're the one who went on a date with her."

"Blaire blackmailed me into a date. She still owes me that hundred bucks."

"And I will pay you as soon as I remember," Blaire said, coming back. She tossed her phone into her purse and pulled out her wallet.

"People in the Arctic can smell your bullshit," I replied.

"Yeah, well, it stinks. What can I say?" She grinned. "Sorry. Gotta go. William's phone stopped working again."

"Did he plug it in?" Aspen asked, raising an eyebrow.

"He says it's connected, so probably not." She put five bucks down on the table to cover her drink, waved, and left.

Aspen waved over the server. "We may as well order."

We did just that, both of us ordering our usual burgers.

"So," she said. "You never did tell me how that date went with the nameless girl."

"Blaire's colleague?"

"Yup."

"It was the worst date of my life."

Her eyebrows shot up. "And you went out with Roxanne Carter in high school."

"Again, Blaire still owes me money for that, too," I said dryly. "I only took her to the movies because Blaire wanted to go out with her boyfriend."

She frowned, then realization washed over her face. "Right, Liam Daniels. Blaire was kind of a bitch."

"She's still kind of a bitch," I said. "But, to be fair, so was Roxanne. She knew Blaire was on a date with Liam and they cheated on each other all the time."

"Did she—wait, no, I don't want to know." She shook her head, her wavy hair flicking over her shoulders.

I laughed.

"Why did you never take anyone out for me?" she asked.

"Because," I said, my tone dry, "I was usually taking you out so you didn't have to go places alone."

She opened her mouth and then closed it. "You enjoyed that."

"Oh, yeah. As a teenage boy, there was nothing I wanted to do more than take out my best friend instead of potentially getting laid."

"Hey, I offered you sex if you took me to prom." She held up her hands. "It's not my fault if you were a gentleman."

"Aspen, we left prom, got drunk on the beach, and you passed out on the way home."

"That's not the point. The offer was there."

Yeah, and when I'd taken her up on it... I shook off the thought.

"What? It was."

I frowned, then stopped. She thought I was shaking my head at her.

Good. The last thing she needed to know was that I was actually thinking about having sex with her.

"What kind of mood is Abuelita going to be in tomorrow?"

"As a rule, a terrible one," I replied, leaning back in the booth and linking my fingers behind my head. I gave her a quick rundown of what had happened last night, starting with Aunt Val calling.

Aspen winced. "Great. They're still not talking to her?"

I unlinked my fingers and held my hands out. "She

divorced a Mexican, is dating a Canadian, and my mom is the one who has to take Abuelita's shit for it all. Of course they're not talking."

"Is it just those two not talking to her?"

"Right now, but she'll probably do something sooner or later and get my dad out of Abuelita's bad books."

"Yeah, right." She laughed. "The day your dad gets out of her bad books depends on who dies first."

I sighed. "That is a sad but incredibly valid point. You'd think, by now, they'd get along."

"Luke, this is your grandmother we're talking about. She barely gets on with herself, never mind anyone else."

"Again, another sad but really fucking valid point."

She smiled wryly, but there was laughter in her eyes, making them brighter than usual. "So, I can expect endless questions about why I'm not married yet, being fed until my stomach pops, and numbers for at least two of your cousins and a friend's grandson."

I paused for a second. "Based upon past experiences… Just run. Now. Go to Mexico. She'll never look for you there."

She laughed, burying her face in her hands. "I'll take her ice-cream."

"She'll only have the toffee one from Betty's, you know that."

"God, she's like an ancient child."

Given that I'd had a similar thought last night, I simply grinned and took another sip of my Coke. "For the record, my current single cousins Abuelita hasn't yet tried to hook you up with are Sebastian, Emmanuel, Ivan, Manuel, and Pedro."

"For the record, your family needs to get some condoms."

I burst out laughing, snorting my soda up my nose. It burned, and I pinched my nose, squeezing my eyes shut tight until it stopped.

"Again," I said quietly, "Valid point. I'll make a note to buy everyone some for Christmas."

"Order online," she muttered, meeting my eyes. "Or you're gonna get a whole lot of funny looks at Target."

I pointed at her, agreeing, right as our food was brought out.

Thank God I was better looking at my single cousins.

TEN

ASPEN

It's Never A Bad Time For Tacos

I LOVED LUKE'S FAMILY.

That needed to be said. His grandmother cooked for me, his mom cut my hair, and his dad once saved me from a handsy guy at the bar.

Not to mention all the cookies I'd stolen while they were on cooling racks through the years.

They were the best kind of family. They were all close, they loved each other, and they were always there for someone when something went wrong.

Except for Luke's aunt.

Valentina had brought that on herself.

Still, that didn't change the fact that they were batshit fucking crazy.

Especially Abuelita.

Her obsession with marrying me off to one of her "nice Mexican grandsons" had begun the day I turned eighteen and could legally get married. It was forever an annoyance of hers that I'd rejected every single option she'd thrown my way.

It wasn't that I didn't like Luke's cousins. No, the entire family was genetically blessed, like they'd stepped right out of a fucking Disney movie or something. It was just like I didn't click with his cousins the way I clicked with Luke.

It was probably because they were forced on me. Kind of like when my dad used to rub our old dog's nose in her poo if she went inside the house.

That was what dating set-ups were like. Being a puppy and getting your nose rubbed in your own shit.

Honestly, for my part, if Abuelita wasn't able to sniff out a lie from a mile away, I'd tell her I'd met someone.

The damn old woman was basically a human bloodhound.

I put my car into park outside Luke's house, blocking in his truck and his dad's at the end of the dirt driveway, and looked at the house. The wooden-brick façade was warmer than the argument I could already hear raging inside.

They had no windows open.

Neither did I.

That's right. They were fighting that loud.

And, as I got out of the car, I wasn't at all surprised to hear that it was Abuelita and Luke's dad.

It was always Abuelita and Luke's dad.

I locked my car and headed toward the front door. Luke opened it before I had a chance to get within a couple feet of the door.

The look on his face was grim, with his thick, dark brows drawn together. "You sure you wanna go in there?"

"As a rule, no." I stuck my fingers in the pockets of my denim shorts and half-smiled. "What are they fighting about now?"

"I didn't get all of it," he continued, making his way down the steps to me. "But there was something about salsa going missing and sticky fingers. Although Abuelita was speaking English, and it sounded a hell of a lot like shitty fingers."

"Both fit." I shrugged.

"Plus, Valentina is here, so my mom is in a worse mood than anybody."

"Why is she here? I thought she was banned from the house?"

"She wants to talk about Elena's birthday. She wants to take her away, but Abuelita is having none of it and wants to throw a big party."

I blinked at him. "Elena's birthday isn't for another four months."

He threw up his arms. "I don't know, but if I hear another thing about it, I'm going to throw myself off the pier and hope a fucking hungry shark finds me."

Laughing, I shook my head. "You don't need to be so drastic. Maybe they'll calm down if I go in there."

"You're still going in there knowing they're fighting?"

"Well, yeah. Abuelita is gonna kick my ass if I don't go in there and see her. Birthday or not."

"That's right. It's your birthday." His eyes sparkled. As if he'd forgotten. "C'mere."

His long strides had the distance between us closed in seconds, and he reached out, grabbing my wrists and pulling me into his firm body, tightly wrapping his arms around me. He hugged me so hard he lifted me right off the ground, making my legs kick.

I squealed.

He laughed.

I wrapped my arms around his neck, hugging him back just as tight. I tried to ignore the warmth that spread through my body and made my cheeks flush, but I couldn't help it.

He slowly lowered me again, loosening his hold just the tiniest bit. With my feet firmly back on the ground, Luke kissed my forehead. His lips were warm and soft, lingering a little too long. The gentle touch sent a shiver across my skin, one that made me stop and take a deep breath.

My hands slid down over his shoulders to his chest.

"Happy birthday, Aspen," he said in a low voice, dipping his head so his blue eyes met mine.

I swallowed the lump that had formed in my throat, then smiled. "Thanks."

The front door swung open behind us, and I jerked away from him. He bit back a chuckle as we both looked toward the person standing in the doorway.

His mom.

She was barely three inches taller than Abuelita, but Gabriela Taylor was one of the most beautiful women in existence. It was no lie. I'd put money on it—if she hadn't gotten married at twenty, she'd have been a beauty queen for years.

She had thick, black hair that hung around and bounced off her shoulders in perfect curls. A mole dotted her skin just beneath her full lower lip—lips that were permanently coated in a dark red that complimented her unfairly smooth olive skin to perfection.

Her eyes were large and dark, surrounded by lashes and framed by brows as thick as the hair on her head.

And those same eyes were currently glittering with amusement as they looked up at me and Luke.

"Did he bite you?" Gabriela looked at me, the lilt of a Mexican accent still tinging her words.

"Pinched me," I lied.

Damn it. I was hoping neither of them had noticed my little flinch and jump move there.

"Right on the arm," Luke continued, lying a hell of a lot more smoothly than I had. "Are they done fighting yet?"

Gabriela turned her gaze to him, one eyebrow slowly raising. "What do you think?"

He sighed.

She pulled the door shut behind her and stepped out barefoot onto the top step. "They were almost done arguing about the damn salsa until Valentina got involved."

"Uh-oh," I muttered.

"Mm," she hummed. "Something about why they couldn't get along, then Mama asked why she couldn't keep it in her pants." She sighed, running her fingers through her hair, leaving it unkempt.

Luke turned to me, smirking. "Are you sure you want to go in there?"

"Your house is a permanent war zone." I tucked my hair behind my ear. "And, as I said, I don't want Abuelita's wrath on me. That woman carries anger like ants carry food."

"Constantly, and with unbelievable strength for such a short person." Gabriela laughed, nodding.

"Says you." Luke patted her on the head, and she responded by standing on her tiptoes and slapping the back of his. He winced, rubbing his ear, and I laughed, following her inside.

"You should know better than that," I shot in his direction with a wide grin.

He mumbled something under his breath, walking behind me, still rubbing his head.

The arguing was intense. It was a psycho mix of Spanish and English, most of it broken English on Abuelita's part.

The perfect English? That was Luke's dad, shouting at the "crazy fucking women" in his house.

It was a good thing they lived a little out of the way and didn't really have any neighbors. Although, to be honest, this was probably why they lived here.

"Enough!" Gabriela shouted, drawing silence from the others in the room.

Abuelita put her hands on her hips. "You let her here!"

Gabriela pinched the bridge of her nose. "I did not. She walked in, madre." She said something in Spanish, something I didn't understand, and then pointed at Valentina who stood in the corner with a scowl on her face.

Much like Gabriela, Valentina was stunningly beautiful, but she was the harder of Abuelita's two youngest children, and it showed in her features.

Gabriela continued on in fluent Spanish, barely taking a breath as she scolded both her mother and her sister. They shouted back, arms waving as the conversation apparently got heated.

Luke grabbed my arm and steered me out of the kitchen, nodding to his dad. "Ignore those. Abuelita will forgive you if she realizes she was acting like a five-year-old when you came to see her...on your birthday."

I nudged him as we stepped back through the front door into the front yard. "Talking of my birthday, where's my present? It's not like you actually forgot."

"Your present will be me delivering you to your apartment and pulling your hair back from your face while you vomit." His tone was dry as we walked to the drive. "What time are we meeting tonight?"

"Stop changing the subject." I paused at my car. "And that's not a present, that's your duty as my best friend. We both know Tom will be doing the same for Blaire."

"Yes," he said slowly, lips quirking. "But Tom's her boyfriend."

"I don't have one of those."

"I'm aware."

"Which means it's your job."

"I don't know how I get myself in these situations." He shook his head and pulled his keys from his pocket. "I was going to give you this later, but since you have the patience of a bonfire near a match..."

I held up my hands. "I can be patient. As long as you tell me what it is."

He shot a look over his shoulder and pulled a small, badly-wrapped present from the backseat. "Here."

I grinned, taking it from him like an excited child. I couldn't help it. I loved presents. It was about the only good thing about my birthday, because it sure as hell wasn't the gift card my parents had tossed into the birthday card they'd mailed...yesterday.

Sitting on the top step, I put the present on my lap and tore into the pink paper. The contents were soft, and as I pulled them out, the black fabric formed into a tank top.

On the front, the graphic read, 'If sarcasm burned calories, I'd be one skinny bitch.'

I ran my tongue over my top lip, slowly turning my head to face him.

Luke leaned against my car with a shit-eating grin spread across his face. It lit his eyes up to an almost impossible blue, and the laughter that was written all over his face and emphasized with his shaking shoulders was almost contagious.

Almost.

I schooled my features into a poker face and met his eyes. "Are you calling me fat?"

His amusement was wiped clean off his features. His grin disappeared so fast his lips formed a small 'o', and his eyes widened like he'd just been caught in headlights—or naked in the town square.

"What?" Luke scratched out, holding out his hands. "No—I just—it's a joke. Because you're sarcastic. Plus it's a small. And—"

I burst into giggles.

"Aspen! Fuck you!"

I laughed even harder, bending over, my stomach hurting from my own stupid prank.

He snatched the paper from my lap, balled it up, and threw it at my head.

Clutching the shirt close to my chest, I got up, running across the dirt drive, past my car, still laughing as I went. Another ball of paper hit me in the back, and it hit me so hard that I almost stumbled over a rock in the drive.

I recovered just in time to set my footing right, but I stopped running, still holding the shirt close. Turning, I held out a hand, wheezing laughter. "I'm sorry! I'm sorry!"

Luke pointed at me. "You're a little shit!"

I grinned. "We've been friends for twenty years. Did you just realize that?"

"No, I knew it when we were eight, and you told Maisie Cooper I had cooties because you knew I liked her and you hated her!"

"Hey, now, she was a bitch!" I held both hands up now. "We were eight!"

"You think a woman's bitch radar has an age limit? Boy, sit down. I could recognize bitches before I could take a shit on a toilet."

His lips twitched with laughter. "That's not the point!"

"That's totally the point. She was a bitch. Don't try telling me your next revelation will be that I'm a bitch."

"I can't say that. It's your birthday."

"Damn right you can't. Tell me you love me instead."

"Over my dead body."

I shrugged. "I watch enough of the Investigation Discovery channel. That could be arranged."

"Ah." He put his hands in his ass pockets and shrugged, looking way hotter than he had any right to. "But, if you kill me, who'll hold your hair back when you vomit tonight?"

Holding out my right arm, I flicked the black band on my wrist. "Fuck diamonds. I've got a girl's best friend right here. A hair tie."

"Your hair tie is your best friend?"

"Yes. It ties back my hair. It's there in emergencies. It can fix bras in a pinch if you know how to. And you know what? My hair tie has never judged me."

"I've seen you tell them to fuck off when they've broken on you."

"Yeah, well some of those are bitches, too. It's not my fault I have thick hair. I didn't ask for this." I sniffed, lowering my arms to my waist. "Thank you for my shirt. I'm wearing it tonight."

He smirked. "Blaire is gonna kill you."

"It's my birthday. I do what I want. If I want to show up in sweatpants and slippers, I will."

"Have you told her that?"

"No. I like to surprise her." Grinning, I walked past him toward my car. I was just opening my mouth to tell him I'd see him later when the front door to his house swung open.

Abuelita ran out of the house, waving her arms. "Aspen! Aspen! You no go! I make tacos!"

"Did she just say tacos?" I asked Luke.

He nodded. "She made three kinds. Just for you."

"You stay!" Abuelita said, her scarlet-red skirt flailing as she shuffled over to me. "You stay for tacos!"

I held a hand to my heart. "Tacos? Do you think I'm crazy? You know the way to my heart, Abuelita. Let's go."

Luke's smile was wide and warm as the tiny woman clutched onto my hand like I was going to disappear. She all but dragged me into the house, babbling about the tacos and salsa and guac she'd made fresh this morning for my birthday.

Tacos.

Abuelita's way of giving you a birthday cake.

I was here for it.

ELEVEN

ASPEN

Tequila Tequila, Shakira Shakira

"YOU HAVE BOYFRIEND?" ABUELITA SAID, eyeing me over the top of her coffee cup.

I wiped my mouth after taking a bite of my hard taco. It was crispy and flavorsome, the shredded chicken inside it seasoned to perfection. "Actually, I—"

"You no lie," she said, barely batting an eyelid as she blew on the hot liquid.

"Am single," I continued, setting the taco down in the fancy holder she had and reaching for my water.

She nodded slowly. "You know Sebastian? He single. Handsome. Good job."

Luke eyed me. "Junior doctor."

I shot him a look that said I wanted to cut off his balls before I turned back to Abuelita. "I do know him, but I—"

"And Pedro—he single now. More handsome than Sebastian." Abuelita didn't stop to listen to me. "Emmanuel just graduated."

"Emmanuel is a little young for me," I said diplomatically, picking my taco back up.

"Ivan single. He like you. You pretty. He handsome. He good job," Abuelita rambled on, taking a spoonful of sugar and putting it in her coffee.

"Ivan is very nice," I replied. "But—I"

"You no like Ivan? Manuel. Manuel is perfect! He is handsome."

Handsome was becoming a theme of this conversation.

"He looking for a good wife like you. You cook?"

"I can cook," I said hesitantly.

"You clean?"

"Until the animals take a cue from Disney, I clean."

"You have children?"

"Abuelita," Luke interjected. "She's being polite. Can't you see that?"

Her eyebrows shot up, and she looked from me to him, before answering in Spanish I didn't understand.

"No," Luke replied in English. "She doesn't want to date Sebastian, or Pedro, or Emmanuel, or Ivan, or Manuel."

She clasped a hand to her chest and looked at me with wide eyes. "You do not?"

Thanks, Luke.

"Not really," I said apologetically. "Honestly, Abuelita, I'm happy to be single."

"I marry at your age," she shot back.

"Yeah, but, someone needs to look after Luke."

She sighed, dropping her hand to cradle her mug. "He need good girl. You marry him."

"No," Luke and I said simultaneously. "We're okay," he continued.

Abuelita sniffed, pushing back on the chair. It squeaked against the wooden floor as she got up and took her coffee into the next room without another word.

Luke shrugged. "Old people. They're weird."

"Yeah, right, that's a good generalization," I said, picking my taco up again. "It's not just that she's fucking crazy."

"Oh, she's fucking crazy." He met my eyes. "Us getting married? As if."

"It's enough with you as my best friend." The snort left me without another thought.

His laugh echoed mine. "Exactly." He got up and kissed the top of my head. "Finish your tacos, Miss Piggy, and I'll see you later."

Flipping him the bird, I shoved the last bite of the taco in my mouth and reached for another.

"I DON'T CARE WHAT SHAKIRA SAYS," I SAID, throwing the skirt across my room. "Hips do fucking lie."

Blaire rolled her eyes, tossing me a pair of skinny jeans from my dresser. "Luke told me you ate six tacos at his place earlier."

I had. I had eaten six tacos, and I didn't regret it one bit.

"Don't judge me," I said, sitting on the edge of my bed. "It's not the tacos fault I'm fat."

"Yeah, you're so fat you could go to Sea World, and they'd want to put you on exhibit," she drawled. "Try saying that when you're not putting on a size six pair of jeans."

I checked the label. "These are an eight."

"Don't be an ass."

"I would, but I am an ass." I hauled the jeans up over my butt and successfully buttoned them. "Ah-ha! My love of tacos will live another day."

Blaire looked pointedly at the button. "But probably

not much longer than that."

I grabbed a cushion from my bed and threw it at her head. "It's my birthday. Isn't there a rule to put your bitch back in its box for today?"

"Yeah, but I think I got bored of that after I texted you this morning." She shrugged, opening my underwear drawer. Pulling out the bra that made my boobs look good, she threw it at me. "Change your bra. This makes the girls look like they want to be there."

"Are you trying to get me laid tonight?"

"Well, one of us has to. My period showed up yesterday, so if I can't…"

"I'm not going to get laid."

"Are you on your period, too?"

"Not anymore, but that's not the point." I changed my bra while her back was turned and she was rifling through my shirts in the closet.

"So, get laid," she replied.

"I don't want to get laid. It didn't work out so well last time, did it?"

At that, she paused before she turned around and looked at me. "You're right. Tom will bring you home tonight in case you get your slut bucket out again."

"My slut bucket?"

"Your vagina," she said without blinking. "Your slut bucket."

"I have never had my vagina referred to as a slut bucket in my life," I replied. "And I don't think I ever want it to be again."

She shrugged. "Keep 'em shut, then. Like my heart."

"Like your heart my left tit. You're head over heels for Tom, and you have been since you laid eyes on him when we were fourteen. Shut up." I took the shirt from her and tossed it on the bed. "I'm wearing this one."

Blaire stared at the shirt Luke had given me earlier today and burst out laughing. "Normally, I'd tell you where to stick it, but that's so good I'm not even gonna say a word. Please tell me you accused him of saying you were fat."

"I did, and it was oh so good. He walked right into it." I pulled the shirt over my head and put my arms through the holes. It fit me perfectly—with just the right amount of give that my over-indulgence in tacos a few hours ago wasn't visible over the waistband of my jeans.

I swear if Luke wasn't straight…

"He'd be a great stylist if he were gay," Blaire mused, glancing at how the shirt fit. "How does he always know to size up for your comfort and up two for my boobs?"

"Probably because I never wear anything skin-tight because of Abuelita's cooking, and you constantly whine about clothing companies never considering women with big boobs."

"They don't, though! Have you seen these things?" She cupped her sizable chest. "You think they make "Size ten plus boobs" for the busty among us? No. And don't even get me started on bikini tops."

"Okay, I won't." I shrugged. I wasn't exactly small-chested, but I wasn't quite the walking weapon Blaire was, that was for sure.

She had the boobs. I had the ass.

Put us together, and we'd scare even the Kardashians.

I stood up and looked over all my angles in the floor-standing mirror opposite my bed. I'd throw on a pair of heels and a nice kimono to keep Blaire happy. It still didn't change the fact that all I wanted to do was put on some sweatpants and watch trashy reality TV, but I was comforted by the fact that nobody in our friend circle had a birthday until the beginning of October now.

My liver would get a break.

Maybe.

Who knew when Blaire would break out a reason to get drunk?

She could do it in her sleep.

And I had no reason to believe she wouldn't pull out

every trick in her little handbook tonight.

And I was more than a little scared about that.

"TO ASPEN!" TOM LEAD THE TOAST, RAISING HIS tequila shot high above his head.

This was shot five.

I wasn't sure I wanted to drink it.

But I would. I was weak-willed, and it really didn't go in my favor that Blaire noticed my hesitation. She reached over, tipping the shot into my mouth before I had a chance to realize what she was doing.

The tequila burned as it went down, and Blaire threw hers back as I wrinkled my face up.

"Ahhh! I wasn't ready!" I shouted, giggling into my hand right after.

"You're good, you're fine, you got this!" Blaire waved her hand, the empty shot glass moving with her. "Just choke it back!"

"That's what she said!" Justin shouted across the table.

I flipped him the bird as I slammed the glass down. There was no lime—I didn't know what to do with myself.

"Yo, Dec!" Will leaned back and waved toward the bar. "Princess over here needs some lime!"

"Princess is gonna kick your bitch ass!" I shouted, grabbing the glass of water from the center of the table.

Declan laughed, holding up a finger. "Y'all give me a minute. The next couple rounds are coming up. Salt, tequila, lime. Perfect for the princess." He cast a glance my way and winked.

"I'm not a princess!" I shouted.

Luke tugged on my hair. "Then why are you wearing a tiara?"

I touched my fingers to the tiara I'd been presented with within seconds of walking through the door. "I was made to. It's not my fault. It was shoved on my little head!"

"Little head? Does that include your ego?" Justin grinned.

I pointed at him. "You. I don't like you."

He laughed, along with everyone else.

"Tequilaaaa!" Blaire shouted, snapping her fingers as Declan presented us with two large, circle bar trays.

Salt. Tequila. Lime.

I didn't know if I could do a sixth.

Jesus.

I hadn't signed up for this.

Luke pushed a tequila shot toward me, complete with the salt shaker and the wedge of lime.

I wrinkled my face up. "I need a vacation from all y'all pushers."

The entire table erupted into laughter—Luke, Blaire, Tom, Justin, Will, Sean.

All it did was teach me that I needed more female friends.

Or maybe not. Women were bitches. Nobody needed more bitches in their lives than absolutely necessary.

Either way...

I already regretted this.

TWELVE

LUKE

Truth Bombs

I WRAPPED MY ARM AROUND ASPEN, HELPING her out of the cab. The driver laughed as she almost tripped over her own feet.

Her bare feet.

I'd stolen her heels an hour ago.

I tossed Declan's brother a twenty for his troubles and closed the door behind us. I knew I'd stayed sober tonight for a reason, and that was because Aspen and Blaire had the self-control of a piece of paper under a running tap.

And I didn't want a repeat of last weekend.

"There's a curb there," I said, stopping just short of it. "You think you can get one foot up on there without falling?"

Aspen stuck her tongue out of the side of her mouth,

narrowing her eyes. She leaned forward so far that the only thing stopping the both of us tumbling over was the fact my upper body strength eclipsed her entire body.

That was a very clear no.

"Jump." I barely bit back a laugh as she leaped onto the sidewalk.

"Ah-ha!" She fist-pumped the air. "Got it!"

Oh, Jesus. It's like she was in Pac-Man or something.

"Okay, you little lush, let's get you to bed."

"I want fooooooood," she said, wrapping her arm around my waist. "Did Abuelita give me quesadilla?"

"Yes," I said slowly, inputting the code for the apartment door and taking her inside. The elevator seemed like a smarter bet right now. "You want me to heat you up some?"

"Mmm, quesadilla." She hiccupped, then giggled.

She was adorable drunk. Seriously—she was so fucking cute. She giggled like a little kid, and her hiccups were so quiet yet forceful.

I pressed the button to her floor as she leaned into me, giggling at seemingly nothing. She was hammered. The only thing that would save her now was, literally, eating her weight in carbs to line her stomach and drinking a pint of water in the hope her body caught up with her good ideas.

Tomorrow was going to be a hoot.

The last time she'd been this drunk she'd turned

twenty-one.

Another night I'd stayed sober, just like she had on my birthday.

What were best friends for?

"Come on, Asp. Let's get you upstairs and out of those jeans."

She snickered. "I'm pretty out of my pants."

"You're pretty in them," I said without thinking. "But I think you'll hate me tomorrow if I let you wear them to sleep."

"I could never hate you." She patted my stomach.

Yeah, well, if she could remember last weekend, she probably would.

The elevator doors opened. I guided her out, then reached for her purse.

She jerked from me, assuming a ninja position with her purse held tight to her body. "Whatchu doin'?"

"Getting your keys," I said slowly. "So I can heat up your quesadillas, Jackie Chan."

She looked at her purse, widening her eyes. "Oh. Quesadilla!" She produced her keys faster than any person who'd consumed their body weight in tequila should have been able to and threw them at me.

On the floor, to be more precise.

Sighing, I bent down and picked up her cluttered ring of keys from the ground in front of my feet. "Yes, quesadilla. You think you can walk from there to the door?"

She held her arms out at her sides to balance her like I was asking her to prove she was sober. Tongue out again, she focused extra-hard on one foot in front of the other until she reached me…

Two feet to the right of where she'd started.

Hey, at least she could walk.

I unlocked her front door and stood aside so she could walk in. She was doing real good until her toes came into contact with a rogue sneaker. That was her undoing. She stumbled over the sneaker, shrieking, falling so fast not even I could catch her.

Aspen landed on the floor with a thud, but fell over, rolling onto her back with a laugh.

Man.

I couldn't wait to tell her those bruises came from a sneaker.

Right now, though, I shook my head and helped her drunk ass up. I was finally able to coerce her to the sofa and pull quesadillas from the fridge to heat up.

Babysitting your drunk best friend was hard work.

Nobody told you that.

Pay your taxes, they said. Pay your rent and your cable and your electric. Make sure your car has insurance.

Nobody ever fucking told me to make sure my best friend could get her drunk ass to bed.

Nope.

Then again, she'd probably felt that way about me a lot of damn times.

Friendship. Never mind through thick or thin. Through sober or tequila should have been the motto.

Aspen arched her back and pulled off her jeans. I paused for barely a second before I returned my attention to the oven and the food I was heating in them.

I was fucking hungry, and whether she was hungry or just alcohol-hungry, she needed to eat.

I didn't want to clean up her vomit tomorrow.

"Luke?" she asked from the sofa, staring at her hand.

"Yeah?"

"Can I have some water?"

Oh, look. Sober Aspen was in there somewhere.

"Sure. Gimme a sec." I pulled a bottle from the fridge and walked to hand it to her. "I even popped the top for you."

"You say that like I'm a chi-ult," she said, eyeing the water bottle.

"Yeah, well, when you can say "child" like the average person, I'll let you open your own water." I hid my laughter as I went back to the kitchen.

She rolled her head back. "That smells good."

"Abuelita's quesadilla. So it should," I said, checking the oven.

"Yum. I'm hungry." She paused. "I drank a lot of tequila tonight, didn't I?"

"You did," I confirmed. "Blaire is a terrible influence on you."

Aspen sighed, sinking into the corner of the sofa. "This is why I wanted to watch movies. No tequila. No wings. No acid reflux." She paused. "No you."

"What the hell is wrong with me?"

Rolling her head to the side, she smiled, but it was sad. "Nothing. Did I tell you that you're perfect?"

"Not today, Asp." I checked the oven and pulled the quesadillas out. Silence reigned as I served them up onto plates and took them over to the coffee table. "You think you can work a knife and fork?"

Aspen glared at me, falling back in the chair. "I'm not a child."

I held up my hands.

She grabbed her quesadilla with two hands, biting into it like it was a burrito.

I was, thankfully, smart enough to not say a word.

So much for not being a child.

We ate in silence, except for Aspen's random hiccups. It took everything I had to hide my laughter each time, mostly because she frowned at her quesadilla like it was to blame.

I only let myself laugh quietly when I took my plate

over to the sink.

"I know you're laughing," Aspen slurred, hiccupping again. "I'm going to write to the tequila company. They broke my diaphu... diaf..."

"Diaphragm?"

"Yes!" She pointed at me, falling over the sofa until she was lying on her stomach. Another giggle and hiccup. "Diaphragm! That's the badger!"

"It's the furthest thing from a badger, Asp."

"Whatever. I'm going to complain. They broke me!"

"No, what broke you is your inability to pace yourself. And eat a decent dinner, because six tacos at two p.m. before you start drinking doesn't make dinner."

She smiled dreamily. "But those were good tacos."

"Yes," I said slowly. "But you were drinking on an empty stomach."

"Nooo. I can still feel the tacos in there. I didn't poop yet!"

I closed my eyes and pinched my nose. I forgot how...fun...she was when I wasn't also drunk. "Well, that was a little too much information."

"Oh no." Her eyes widened, and she stumbled to sit up. "Was my poop supposed to be a secret?"

"I'd prefer it to stay that way." I walked over and held out my hands. "Come on. I think you should go to bed now. Sleep off those hiccups."

She giggled, yet another hiccup interrupting it, and put her hands in mine. She was definitely unsteady on her feet, so I gave up with the hands and wrapped my arm around her again.

"Secrets are fun." She leaned right into me, making me stagger against the doorframe.

"Fucking hell, woman. At least try to put one foot in front of the other."

"Oh. Right. Sorry." She dropped her chin and stared at her feet. Her tongue poked right out of the side of her mouth, and she bit down on it, carefully putting her right foot in front of her left.

We were going to be here all night.

"All right. Come here." I stopped us both, then bent down, hooking one arm behind her knees and lifting her up.

She hiccupped, then burst out laughing, holding onto my neck. I hauled her over to the bed and set her down.

"I'm gonna help you take your jeans off, okay?" I looked down at her.

Aspen pushed hair from her face and propped herself up on her elbows. Her eyes were wide, staring at me like I'd just kicked her puppy. "You're going to take off my jeans?"

"Do you want to sleep in them?"

Her shoulders shook, then, well. Then, she laughed her fucking ass off.

I blinked at her.

"You're going to take my jeans off!" She whispered, covering her mouth with her hand. "Ohhhh! Is it going to happen again?"

"Is what going to happen again?"

"Ssshhhhhh. Nothing. It's a secret!" She tapped her finger against her lips in a "shh" motion. She did that for another few seconds before she reached down and undid the button of her jeans.

I frowned but said nothing. I helped her peel the skin-tight jeans down her legs and over her feet. Tossing them on the floor, I reached over her and pulled the covers back.

Aspen yawned. "Oh. It's not happening again. Good."

Still holding the covers, I said, "What isn't happening?"

She looked around the room, honey-colored eyes darting back and forth. "I can't tell you."

"Then stop talking about it."

"I can't!" She gasped, covering her mouth again. "But I can't say. No. It's a secret."

"Okay. That's the tequila talking." I tucked the covers up over her and turned off the light on her nightstand. "Goodnight, Asp."

"You're going?"

"I'm going to sleep on the sofa. I don't want to be vomited on by you later." I smiled.

"Will you stay if I tell you?"

"Tell me what?"

"The secret," she whispered conspiratorially. "But you can't tell Luke."

I opened my mouth to remind her that I was Luke but stopped.

I wanted to know what in the ever-loving fuck the crazy shit was talking about.

"I won't tell Luke," I said slowly.

She snuggled right under the covers and patted the bed next to her. When I sat down, she said, "Do you promise you won't tell him?"

"I won't tell him a thing. Promise," I replied.

Well, I wasn't fucking breaking it, was I? It wasn't like I could tell myself a secret.

"Okay. Okay." She took a deep breath. "Last weekend, I had really bad drunk sex with Luke."

Fuck.

"Like, really bad." She paused. "And I can't tell him, because he doesn't remember, and he's my best friend."

Fuck.

"And it's awkward," she sing-songed, sounding even more tired. "Because he's kind of hot," she sighed. "And I had a dirty dream…"

Wait—what?

"Where it was better than tap-tap-squirt…" she

finished on a yawn.

I waited, but she didn't say anything else. "Aspen?"

A tiny snort answered me, and when I peered over, her eyes were closed. She smacked her lips together, licking the lower one, and stilled.

She'd passed out.

And there was no fucking way I was going to be able to sleep tonight.

SHE REMEMBERED.

She remembered that night, and so did I, and now our friendship was irrevocably fucking changed.

There was no way she'd forget what she'd said last night. There was no way I could move on like she hadn't said a thing. I had to tell her what she'd told me and admit that I remembered last weekend, too.

If I didn't, the secret might just be the one thing that killed our friendship.

It was fine when I didn't think she knew. It was easier before. I could move on from that bad night, and any lingering thoughts I had about her beyond being my best friend would die eventually.

Now?

No.

Now, it was different. There was no going back from here.

I rested my forehead against the top of the island and clasped my fingers behind my neck. The island was cool against my skin, and it was soothing. Thank fuck something was because my stomach was in knots.

I reached for my phone and looked at the time. I had a new message from Blaire.

BLAIRE: Is Aspen awake yet?

ME: No. Thank fuck.

BLAIRE: Why? Did she try to striptease for the building manager again?

ME: No, but you nearly showed the bar a second full moon.

BLAIRE: Eh. I was just giving them the perspective of an alien on another planet. What's up?

I ran my fingers through my hair. If Aspen remembered, that meant Blaire already knew about last weekend.

Fuck knew I needed to talk to someone about this.

ME: She told me what happened last weekend. She was so drunk she thought I was someone else.

BLAIRE: Fuck.

BLAIRE: Um, I don't know what else to say.

ME: I remembered, Blaire. I didn't think she did so I didn't say anything.

BLAIRE: LOL WHAT? YOU REMEMBERED?

Well, someone had to be able to laugh about this shit. It sure as hell wasn't going to be me anytime soon.

ME: How the hell is this funny?

BLAIRE: Are you telling me you've both been walking around for the last week, knowing you've had sex, but pretending you didn't remember?

ME: Admitting that I lasted two minutes isn't on my bucket list.

BLAIRE: Eh, you were drunk. Tom can't even get it up when he's drunk that much tequila. You're already winning.

Awesome. That was what I wanted to know.

ME: I don't need to know about his penis. I need your help.

BLAIRE: You have to talk about it. It's not a big deal, Luke. It happened. It was bad. You were drunk. It was a mistake. You can both admit that and move on.

ME: It's just not that simple. She's my best friend.

BLAIRE: So fuck her properly to get it out of your systems and move on after that.

ME: That's your solution? Fuck her again?

BLAIRE: Sober this time.

ME: That's not helpful.

BLAIRE: That's all I got. I'm hungover. Try again later.

I sighed and turned my phone over. She was no help. Not that I'd expected her to be.

Rubbing my hand down my face, I pushed up off the stool and went to get water from the fridge. I grabbed a second bottle for Aspen and found the bottle of Aspirin in the drawer. I popped her two pills, then two for myself.

Not because I was hungover.

I just had the world's worst stress headache.

I tossed back the pills and washed them down.

And sighed again.

Fuck. I had no idea how to handle this. The conversation had to happen, but how? How? How the fuck did I tell her what she'd said unless she brought it up?

Her bedroom door swung open, and I turned just in time to see a flash of brown hair dart into the bathroom.

I guessed I was about to find out.

When she was done throwing up.

THIRTEEN

ASPEN

A Hangover, A Window, And A Cushion

I WAS DYING.

That was the only explanation for this feeling. My stomach was clenching, my head was pounding, and despite having just vomited for the third time, my tongue felt fuzzy—like someone had glued cotton balls to it.

I sat back from the toilet, using my hand to shield myself from the brightness coming in through the window. The first thing I had to do was flush the toilet and get the vomit off my damn teeth.

Hauling myself up was nearly impossible. I swear my head weighed more than my ass did—at least, it felt that way. I only just managed to brush my teeth without throwing up.

God, I felt awful.

I really should have eaten again before drinking. The tacos at around two were not enough. Not when Blaire is leading the drinking proceedings.

Very, very carefully, I grabbed my robe from the back of the door and tugged it on, loosely tying the belt around my waist. God knew I didn't need any pressure on my stomach right now.

Luke's smirking face was the first thing I saw when I walked out of the bathroom.

"Don't," I croaked, holding up a finger. "Don't even go there."

"Water. Aspirin. On the counter." He nodded toward the bottle with condensation running down the side of it.

"Thank you." I gingerly made my way over to the island, opened the bottle, and downed the pills with a few mouthfuls of water. I shuddered as I swallowed.

It did not feel good.

"How are you feeling?" Luke asked, looking way too smug behind his hand.

"Don't shout," I whispered. "You're very loud."

"No, you're just very hungover," he replied. "And I'm not surprised. You were hammered."

I groaned and leaned against the counter in front of the sink. "I don't remember a thing past, what? Nine? Nine-thirty?"

His eyebrows shot up. "What's the last thing you

remember?"

"Blaire got a round of Tequila Sunrise, but you didn't want yours, so I double-fisted them." I rubbed my hand over my forehead as if it would alleviate the pain that thumped there. "How did we get back here?"

"Declan's brother. He brought us back around eleven."

"Eleven? Dear God."

Luke nodded, lips twitching. "You were really drunk. We came back, and you were hungry."

Quesadilla.

I snapped my fingers. "You heated up Abuelita's quesadillas!"

"Yep. And you ate it with your fingers."

I wondered why my finger was sore. A quick glance at it confirmed I had a small burn on the side of my left middle finger. "That explains the blister."

He looked at me pointedly. "Is that all you remember?"

Was there something I needed to remember?

Dear God. What if we'd had sex again? What if I vomited on him during it? I couldn't ask that, could I? Jesus, this was wrong. This was fucking up.

"Um, did I do something I should remember?" I tried to keep my tone light and breezy, but it came out a little too hesitant for that.

"Yes." He nodded firmly.

Frowning, I took another swig of water. "Did I flash

anyone?"

"No. Only me when I helped you take off your jeans."

So that was how that happened. "Oh, God, I didn't give Justin my number, did I?"

He laughed. "No, Aspen, you didn't give Justin your number. I'd never let you do that."

"Thank God. I didn't make out with anyone, did I?"

"No making out."

I frowned again. I had no idea what I could have done. Flashing my boobs and making out with a bad choice of a guy was my usual go-to. If I'd done something else, I was stumped.

Mind you, racking my brains wasn't working in my favor. I couldn't remember anything except the quesadillas.

Huh.

The quesadillas.

They felt like they were important.

"Doin' okay over there, Einstein?" Luke smirked again.

"The quesadillas. Are they important?"

"You're getting warmer. Keep thinking."

"Can't you just tell me?"

He shook his head. "Oh no. This is on you. Try to remember."

I sighed. I had too much of a hangover for this. "Okay. You made quesadillas. I had the hiccups!"

"Yep. Let me know how that letter to the tequila

company for "breaking your diaphragm" goes."

Shit.

I'd said that.

I closed my eyes. "Will do, smartass, will do."

He laughed. "Carry on."

"Did I fall over?" I tilted my head to the side. "Trip over something?"

"Your own feet."

"Right. You put me to bed. Pulled off my jeans. I remember now." I was getting close. "I asked you something about doing it again."

I had a bad feeling about this.

He nodded, his messy hair flicking back and forth. "You were very, very adamant you couldn't tell me what you meant by that, so I tucked you in and turned off your light."

Oh no.

I was remembering.

"And then I said I'd tell you if you promised not to tell Luke." I was frozen. I couldn't move. Except for my heart. That was running a fucking marathon inside my ribs. "And you promised."

"And then," he said slowly, his intense gaze holding mine, "You told me that you and I had had really, really bad sex last weekend."

The water bottle slipped out of my hand. Kaput. Right

to the floor, where it exploded, spraying water all over the floor and the cabinets.

"Oh God," I breathed.

And then I'd told him I couldn't tell him because of our friendship.

And that I'd had a dirty dream about him.

Oh.

Fucking.

Hell.

Slowly, I brought my hands to my face, covering my mouth and nose when all I really wanted to do was climb up onto the kitchen counter, open the window, and haul myself out of my fourth-floor apartment.

Yup.

My head hurt enough that it wouldn't matter. The asphalt sidewalk might just finish me off. I was going to die of embarrassment anyway.

"Oh no," I whispered into my hands, the gentle sound being muffled.

Luke grimaced, rubbing the back of his neck. "I have a confession to make."

"Go ahead. This can't get much worse." I dropped my hands, only to bring them back up and fist my hair.

"I remembered."

What? "What?"

"Last Saturday." He scratched behind his ear, glancing

away from me for a second. "I remembered it. I didn't know how to bring it up, and when you made up that story, I just figured you couldn't remember and made up something random."

I shook my head. Once. I really couldn't do that much.

"Obviously, now I know that you made it up because you didn't want to bring it up."

"I thought you'd forgotten!" I said, my voice a little too shrill. Like a villain in a Disney movie. "You asked me what happened, and I panicked! I was never supposed to admit it. Oh, my God. Oh, my God."

I pushed off the counter and walked into the living room. This wasn't happening, was it? It had to be a drunken dream. I was still drunk. Still sleeping. In my room.

I hadn't really told him that, had I?

I had. Oh, God. I had.

I'd told him we'd had really bad sex.

This was the worst day of my life.

I turned to face him.

"If it makes you feel better, I'm under no illusions about how bad that sex was for you," Luke said, spinning on the stool. "Only pornstars cum in two minutes, and that's because of smart editing."

I couldn't help the tiny laugh that left me, even though my cheeks burned. "I'm sorry."

"For what? I'm the one, who, to use your words, was a

tap-tap-squirt."

Oh, God, it could get worse.

I sank onto the sofa, burying my face in a cushion. "Oh, Goddddd."

He didn't say anything, and neither did I. I could barely breathe with my face this far into the cushion, but it didn't really matter. I didn't want to breathe. I wanted to disappear.

I didn't think I could feel worse when I'd woken up twenty minutes ago.

How, how naïve I'd been. To go back to vomiting in the toilet. That was better than this. So much better.

I took a deep breath and lifted my head to see Luke standing behind the sofa with another bottle of water in his hands.

"Here," he said. "You need to rehydrate, or you'll feel worse."

"There is literally no way I could feel worse than I do right now," I said, taking the bottle. "Not a chance in hell. I'd bet my bank account on it."

"That's not really a whole lot, is it?"

"My savings account." Which was sitting at a tidy three-and-a-half thousand dollars, thank you very much.

"Oh, well, then you're right. You probably can't." He shrugged his wide shoulders and perched on the arm of the sofa.

Opposite end to me.

I drank some of the water, then recapped the bottle and looked down at the cushion on my lap. I couldn't believe I'd gotten so drunk I hadn't even known who he was.

That I'd been so drunk, I'd told him the one thing I swore to myself I never would.

Now what the hell did we do?

This wasn't a secret anymore. We couldn't just pretend it never happened.

"Now what?" Luke asked.

"I don't know. It's not like we can pretend it never happened." I paused. "There's an elephant in the room, and unlike you, I have a feeling it's going to last longer than a couple minutes."

His lips thinned out into one flat line. "You know that was because of the tequila, right?"

I shrugged.

"Your subconscious knows."

Oh, look. I could feel worse.

"Give me your bank details," I muttered, my cheeks flaming red-hot. "I'll just transfer you my savings."

He laughed behind his hand.

He knew about the sex. He knew about my dirty dream. Thank God he didn't know it'd happened the night he'd stayed here.

"If it makes you feel better—"

"If it follows the theme of the morning, it won't," I drawled.

"Probably not," he agreed. "But I've had at least two dirty dreams about you since it happened."

"Aren't we supposed to be making this less awkward?"

"Well, keeping secrets hasn't exactly worked in our favor this week, has it?" He got up and walked over to the coffee machine. "Coffee?"

"Can you lace it with arsenic?"

"I can, but it probably wouldn't taste that good." Shrugging, he pulled down two mugs and set to it. "Look, Asp, it happened. Neither of us have to keep it a secret anymore. That's a good thing."

Yeah, well, it was a good thing for him. He'd gotten an orgasm out of it. I'd gotten nothing but disappointment and embarrassment.

Ah. The life of a twenty-something female looking for love.

Disappointment and embarrassment.

They didn't tell you that when they told you it was time to grow up.

"I don't know," I murmured. "I kinda preferred it when it was a secret."

"Shit." He switched the mugs out and looked over at me. "It's awkward, isn't it?"

"What, me knowing that you know that you're the

worst sex of my life? Not at all. It's a fucking delight."

"Wow. Tell me how you really feel about it."

"I'm sorry. Your two minutes of banging me like a drum were the best of my life."

"There's no need to be so sarcastic."

"Then fuck off," I muttered. "I'm too hungover for this. And embarrassed. So embarrassed." I buried my face in the pillow again.

There was a silence for a moment and then, "I should probably leave right now, huh?"

I nodded, not lifting my head. "Please do."

"All right. But this conversation isn't over, Aspen. Not by a long shot."

And that was what I was afraid of.

BLAIRE PICKED THROUGH THE POPCORN bowl, looking for the biggest pieces.

I hadn't eaten all day. I hadn't been able to. It'd taken another nap and more pills than I cared to admit before I was able to stomach anything but water. I'd even thrown out the coffee Luke had made before he'd left.

Between my hangover and my admission last night— and the subsequent conversation—I didn't have the appetite anyway.

I was too hung up on the fact Luke knew he was the worst sex I'd ever had.

And that he'd known it before I'd ever admitted it.

I hadn't processed this yet. In fact, I was at the point where I was willing to avoid him for the rest of my life. Maybe move to a remote town in Montana.

Or Alabama. My Texas heart couldn't cope with the cold in Montana.

Alabama would work.

A piece of popcorn hit me on the cheek and bounced down to the floor. I turned to Blaire who was staring at me with one eyebrow raised.

"Well?" she asked, holding a piece of popcorn between her finger and thumb. "What are you going to do about it?"

"Move to Alabama," I answered without thinking.

"I see where you're going with this, but no, sorry. I need you here. Alabama is too far."

"New Mexico?"

"You ain't even goin' to Dallas," she shot back. "You aren't moving. You can't afford it."

"I have money in my savings." Although, if Luke ever called in that bet, I was fucked with a capital F.

"Oh, my God. Grow a pair, Aspen!" Blaire put the bowl on the coffee table and pulled the blanket we were sharing a little tighter to her waist. "Boohoo. Luke knows y'all fucked and it was bad. Newsflash, it's not like you told him it happened. He knew anyway!"

I folded my arms across my chest. I already knew they'd spoken, and I'd have been pissed if she didn't love him as much as I did.

You know, as a friend.

"I'm gonna tell you what I told him. Suck it up and accept it as a mistake and move on or whip off your panties and fuck for real."

"I don't think either of those are an option," I replied slowly.

"Then get your ass back to school and become a fucking astronaut," she shot back without blinking. "He's been your best friend longer than I have. Are you really gonna let one drunken mistake ruin twenty years of that?"

"It's not just that. I've had…dreams…and apparently, I told him that."

She spat out her Coke. "Shut up!"

"Oh, it gets better. Worse." I paused. "He's had them, too."

Now, she choked.

That's right.

On her own spit.

That was a special kind of skill.

"There's no coming back from this, Blaire. Our friendship is doomed. My life as I know it is doomed."

She blinked at me, then grabbed her phone. "I'm ordering you a pizza. You're dumb when you're hungry."

I grabbed a pillow and screamed into it. It felt good. A bit of the frustration I'd felt since the truth had whacked me in the face this morning left me, evaporating into the air around me.

Thank God.

I'd had the worst headache all day, and while this morning's had been down to tequila, it was now down to stress.

Stress because tequila. And bad choices.

"Right. Pizza ordered." Blaire put her phone on the coffee table and snuggled back under the blanket. "And you're going to listen to me. You can avoid Luke all you want, but you have to talk to him, Aspen. Regardless of how you feel or what happened, you can't leave it like this forever. The only reason you didn't talk to him about it before was that you were afraid to lose his friendship. Well, I'm telling you right now: Talk to him, or you will lose him."

I sighed, hugging the cushion tight.

I knew she was right. This whole situation existed because of my fear of losing my best friend.

Except now, I was afraid that would happen no matter what I said or did.

FOURTEEN

ASPEN

Drama Is Better On TV

I SERVED THE TRAY OF TEQUILA SHOTS TO THE laughing bachelorette party in the corner. They had the longest table in the place, and this was their third round. I was half-expecting them to bust out the old karaoke machine in the corner.

At least they had food. We rarely served it, but they were making their way through grilled cheese and chicken wings like total champs.

Not to mention the roughly ten bowls of chips and salsa I'd placed on their table.

Drunk chicks could eat.

Then again, I knew that. I, myself, was an excellent drunk eater.

"Can I get y'all anything else?" I asked, smiling at

them all.

The bride-to-be beamed at me. "Maybe some water?"

"Sure thing. Would you like ice and lemon with that?"

"Can you bring the lemon on the side?"

"No problem. I'll get y'all a couple jugs and bring it right over." With another smile, I turned and headed back to the bar. I motioned to Mr. Gomez to give me a second while I got the water, and he responded with a warm smile. He was here late, celebrating with his wife—his daughter was pregnant, he'd told me earlier, and that was cause for breaking his steadfast routine.

I couldn't help but agree.

I fixed the party their water, making sure to add extra ice and putting the lemons on a small side plate as they'd asked. It took some serious balance skills to not drop the two trays holding everything, but I managed it.

Going back to the bar, I gave Mr. Gomez his bill. "And congrats, Grandpa!"

He grinned, his slightly crooked teeth adding a ton of character to his already lively personality. "Thank you. I couldn't be more thrilled. Here you go, Aspen, and thank you for the free drinks."

"Free drinks? Who's giving out free drinks?" Declan stepped out to the bar behind me.

"That would be me." I held up my hand.

"I'm gonna be a pappy!" Mr. Gomez exclaimed, smile

still planted on his weathered face.

Declan grinned, leaning past me to shake his hand. "Well, congrats, my friend! I suppose I'll let her off for giving away my best beer for free."

I rolled my eyes and turned to the register. "You're such a drama queen."

"King," he rectified. "I'm a man."

"Fine, be a king." I shrugged. "History dictates that queens were more powerful, but whatever."

"Women." Dec shook his head. "Best hope that baby is a boy, Mr. Gomez."

"All I'm hopin' is that it's healthy and grows up to be as much of a pain in the ass as Gabby was," Mrs. Gomez said, joining him at the bar. "Come on, honey, we've got to go. Family Feud re-runs start in fifteen minutes, and I didn't set the DVR."

I dipped my head to hide my smile. "Your change."

"Keep it." She winked at me. "Buy yourself a pretty dress to find you a husband with."

Three dollars wouldn't get me far, but I laughed and took their empty glasses off the bar. "I'll keep that in mind, Mrs. Gomez. Thank you."

"They'd have to be one hell of a patient husband."

The glasses I was holding slipped, shattering into thousands of little shards as they hit the floor.

I drew in a deep breath before I'd even turned to look

at Luke. He was standing at the bar, leaning forward, biceps pressing against the sleeves of his white t-shirt.

Honestly, it was unfair.

Nobody should have looked that good in a plain white t-shirt.

Between the dark hair and the tanned skin and the toned biceps... yeah, no. Who did I submit a complaint about ridiculous good looks to? Was God accepting those?

Not that he'd listen to me. He and I hadn't been on great terms since my hamster died when I was seven. I'd never really forgiven him for that.

"You all right, Aspen?" Dec eyed me.

"Fine. Luke scared me, is all." I leaped over the broken glass to reach for the dustpan and brush. "It'll only take a second to clean up." I snatched the cleaning stuff from under the bar and got onto my knees to sweep up the glass.

It took me a few minutes, during which Dec and Luke had a casual conversation about football that I tuned right out of. The glass clinked as I tipped the dustpan into the trashcan.

"Hey. Sorry." I stood and tucked a wisp of hair behind my ear. "What's up?"

Luke's lips twisted to the side. "That's what I came to ask you."

Ah. Right. That missed call and three ignored texts would do that. He hated being ignored. Much like a four-year-old.

Dec shot me a confused look.

"Sorry. My phone was dead." I shifted on the spot.

Luke's smirk knew.

Why the fuck was I lying to him? That was like saying you didn't eat the cookies with chocolate all around your mouth.

"Do you have a break coming up soon?" he asked, glancing at Dec. "I only need ten minutes."

I hesitated.

Dec nudged me in the back. "Take your break. I've got the bride squad over there. You've got twenty minutes, all right?"

Great. Just great.

I needed to move to New York City to avoid someone. It just didn't work here.

I took a deep breath and nodded for Luke to follow me. I walked right through the bar right to the outdoor patio, taking a moment to pause to turn on the fairy lights that illuminated the covered area.

Declan's grill area took up one corner, the fuel from last weekend's Fourth of July party still sitting in the bag next to it.

I perched against the table on one of the benches, gripping the edge of the wood. Looking at him was awkward, so I stared at his knees until I could get the words out of my mouth.

His knees.

I know.

What the fuck?

"So… What's up?"

"My knees are flattered you asked," Luke retorted. "But you know what's up."

I gripped the wooden slats a little tighter. "Do we have to have this conversation right now?"

"Yes. I told you—we're talking about this, Aspen. You've ignored me all day, so I came to you."

There was a big ass lump in my throat that made swallowing really hard.

"I'm at work," I replied. "I don't have the time for this right now."

"You either talk to me right now, or I'll wait for you to finish." His eyes met mine with a fire that burned brightly. He was serious. "Dec said we've got twenty minutes, and we're going to use them."

"You know my break is for me to pee and drink and get a snack, right?"

The look he leveled on me said he really didn't care.

I supposed I'd brought this on myself. If I hadn't been a total wet wipe about all of this, I'd be eating chips and salsa right now.

"Fine." I rolled my shoulders. "Say what you need to."

Glancing over his shoulder, he checked the door to the back area was closed. The bar wasn't busy enough for anyone to come back here, and the smoking area Dec had designated was out the front.

Luke scratched the back of his neck and brought his gaze back to meet mine. "I'm sorry I didn't tell you I remembered. I asked you if you knew what happened because I hoped like fuck you didn't remember, and when you fed me that bullshit story, I really thought you'd forgotten."

"I wish I had."

"Not as much as I do. Trust me, Asp, that night was… unfortunate," he continued. "And not because of the fact we had sex, but because of how fucking bad it was. Like, that was the stuff of nightmares. I've gotten myself off in the shower and lasted longer than that."

I sucked in my lower lip and bit down on it so I didn't laugh.

"But it was you. You're my fucking best friend. I couldn't ever imagine doing anything to destroy our friendship, and I swear to God I did that last weekend."

I opened my mouth to reply, but he held his hand up.

"Let me finish," he said. "I was ready to get over it. I accepted you'd forgotten. You had no reason to lie to me, and you didn't, not really. We both kept it a secret for a reason."

Yup.

He ran his hand through his hair. "Shit—I could even get over thinking about you differently, you know? Not just as my best friend, but as someone I'm fucking stupidly attracted to. Someone I think about more than I have any right thinking about."

Oh, God.

This was it.

This was where twenty years of friendship went to shit.

"Then your drunk ass mouth went and ran a marathon on me."

"That's the most accurate description of Drunk Me that I've ever heard," I replied.

He held out his hands. "I've got several years of descriptions if you want them."

"Not really. I think this one is horrific enough right now."

His lips twitched to the side, and I hated how it made my heart flutter a little too much.

"Seriously, Aspen. Your mouth runs faster than Usain Bolt. Especially when you've been drinking, and now I can't stop fucking thinking about what you said to me."

I shifted. Squirming, almost. "Really? I wish I could forget."

"Tell me one thing." Luke took a step toward me. "Do you see me the same way you always did?"

"Honestly, I can't get your weird sex face out of my mind."

"Aspen."

"Have you ever seen it? It's like a cross between Shrek and the Grinch, just a little less green."

"Aspen…"

"Just as hairy, depending on when you last shaved." I paused. "Was that not the right answer? Do I not get to pass Go and collect two hundred dollars?"

"Aspen!"

"No!" I ran my fingers through my hair until they linked at the back of my neck. I met his eyes, slowly letting my hands fall away until they were flat on the table again. My fingers curled around the edge like holding onto it was a lifeline for me. "No, I don't see you the same way anymore."

His throat bobbed, and he nodded. "How do you see me?"

I couldn't tell him I wanted more, could I? I couldn't tell him just how thoroughly I'd thought about his hands moving over my body. I couldn't tell him how I wanted to know if his fingers in my hair felt as good as I thought they would.

I couldn't tell him I'd literally dreamed about his lips and how good he'd kiss me if only I'd let him.

I couldn't tell him that the thought of his lips on mine

made my heart skip a little faster.

Nope.

"I don't know," I whispered, my stomach clenching tight.

"Is that you not knowing because you don't know, or because you don't want to tell me?"

"Both?"

"I figured as much." He took a deep breath, drawing it in before slowly letting it out. His nostrils flared on his exhale, and the intensity in his gaze made me pause.

There was something new there.

I'd seen laughter. Amusement. Bemusement. Disbelief. Shock.

I'd never seen this. Not this darker flicker of emotion I wasn't familiar with seeing in his eyes. It was deeper... Stronger. Something that grabbed hold of me and made sure I couldn't look away.

Like a puzzle I wanted to complete.

A riddle I needed to figure out.

There was a side of my best friend I'd clearly never met—but I had the feeling I was about to.

"Don't hate me," Luke said, eyes on mine. "Okay?"

"If I don't hate you after last weekend, I'd be hard-pressed to now."

"Aspen. I'm being serious. This isn't me messing with you. Just promise me you won't hate me for this."

"For what?"

"This."

His long legs closed the distance between us in seconds. My heart thundered against my ribs. This wasn't normal—he was Luke, my best friend, my rock, my person.

Why was he coming to me?

My answer came in seconds.

His large hand with its roughened fingers from working all day went to the side of my neck. He brushed his thumb over my cheek, his hand cupping the side of my jaw.

He didn't hesitate.

Luke touched his lips to mine.

And he didn't just press them there.

No.

He kissed me.

Kissed me.

His grip on my head was firm. His lips moved expertly over mine. His body became one with mine, and I couldn't help the way I reached out and gripped his t-shirt.

I wanted him closer.

Always closer.

It was the kind of kiss that made your head spin. From confusion and conflict and the thought that although it shouldn't be, it felt like it was right. Meant to be. Like it was a kiss that was filled with all the kind of things a kiss should be.

My best friend kissed me the way a girl should be kissed. Thoroughly, with passion and the kind of heart-clenching magic that was reserved for movies and fairytales.

My best friend.

Luke.

Luke Taylor, the boy who promised me cooties were real and that he'd slay the monsters under my bed was now a man, and he was kissing me.

And boy, that man could kiss.

Everywhere. I felt it everywhere. His kiss was pure magic. Straight-up ecstasy. The tingles that started at my lips cascaded over my skin until every part of my body was alive with his touch.

Dammit.

I was torn. So torn. Into a thousand pieces. Even that wasn't enough.

I curled my fingers into the collar of his shirt and pulled back. I didn't want it to stop. I wanted him to carry on fucking kissing me and take me right here, right now on this damn bench.

But this was scary.

The way he exhaled against my lips told me he felt the same.

It was fucking terrifying.

"You're my best friend," he whispered. "And I can't lose you, Aspen. But I can't ignore the fact you're driving me fuckin' insane, either."

"Then maybe you shouldn't," I replied, my voice barely louder than his.

The door to the patio slammed open. "Aspen! I can't take these women anymore. It's been ten minutes, and they're singing 'It's Raining Men' on the old karaoke machine. How much have they had to drink?" Declan demanded from the doorway.

Luke took a step back from me, and I pushed myself off the bench, darting to the side of his body.

Declan paused. "You've still got ten minutes. You're good."

"It's fine." I wiped my hands on the skin-tight black skirt I was wearing. "I can handle them. We're done here."

My boss looked between us both with a glint in his eye. "You sure?"

"I'm sure." I didn't look back at Luke as I made my way back into the building. "Thanks. I got this."

FIFTEEN

LUKE

Variety Is The Spice Of Life

I WATCHED ASPEN GO, RUNNING BACK INTO the bar like I'd lit a firework and shoved it up her ass, all too aware of Declan's eyes sliding their way toward me.

He'd seen it. I knew he had. There was no way the greying, slightly pot-bellied beer expert hadn't. Even if he hadn't been looking right at us, he wouldn't have missed it.

Slowly, he raised one eyebrow. "Best if I don't say anything, huh?"

Grimacing, I nodded. "It's complicated."

"Women always are, son. I've been married thirty years and still haven't figured her out." He shook his head. "You'll figure it out."

"I hope you're right." I paused. "I don't know what'll happen if we don't."

Dec let the door shut behind him and walked over to me. He rested his hand on my shoulder, squeezing it lightly. "Listen to me, son. There ain't no such thing as an easy relationship. Friendships, romantic ones—it doesn't matter. But I do know this: the only relationships worth having are the ones that are tough."

"Sounds like a damn good reason to stay single for the rest of my life."

"Your grandma ain't gonna be around to cook for you forever, boy."

"I'll live in an apartment over Aspen's garage when she meets someone she'll marry."

He laughed, leaning against the bench the way Aspen just had. "Yeah, I'm sure you will. While you watch her happy and in love and making a future for herself. What I just saw definitely lends weight to that plan."

I blew out a deep breath and ran my fingers through my hair. "All right, maybe that doesn't work for me right now."

"It's never gonna work for you. I don't have to be a bonafide genius to see that you've got some feelin's for my girl."

"Yeah, well, neither does she, considering I just kissed her."

"Finally," Declan replied. "She's been mopin' around here all day in a foul-ass mood. I'd have asked her if she needed a tampon if my wife hadn't taught me better than that."

I laughed, dropping my chin. Yep. I'd been there.

"Can this old man give you one piece of advice?"

"You've already given me some," I replied.

"All right, so I wanna give you a little more, you fuckin' smartass."

My lips twitched into a smile, and I looked at him. "Bite me, old man. Go on."

"I'd bite you if I thought these gnashers could do any damage." He chuckled. "All right, here goes."

"Sounds like you're about to send me on a rollercoaster."

"You're 'bouta send yourself on one, son," Dec retorted. "Here's the one thing you need to know before you take this further. And let me tell you, it ain't easy being married. It ain't easy being single. Not much in life is easy, that's for sure."

I fidgeted. I knew that already. Nothing about being best friends with Aspen had ever been easy—never mind the last week.

"But one thing is for sure," he continued. "Love is easy. Deceptively so. Loving someone is one of the easiest things you can do in your life, but putting that love into action? That's the hard part. Telling someone you love them is terrifying. Reminding them you love them can be an uphill trek. Proving you love them can be something else altogether."

"You're not selling me on relationships here, Dec."

He patted me on the shoulder, standing up. "Love is easy. Relationships are hard. But, if you love someone enough, nothing is ever too hard to fight for."

"I don't love Aspen."

"Ah, that's right. You kids these days kiss for fun. Back in my day, kisses meant something."

Yeah, well, that kiss meant something.

It meant I'd potentially just fucked up twenty years of friendship.

Dec slapped me on the back and stood up. "You'll figure it out, kid. You've got too much between you to let it slip away. Be honest, and you can't ever do wrong."

With that, he left me alone on the patio.

I couldn't help but think he was wrong.

Aspen's drunken truths were why we were here in this situation.

Sometimes, the truth did nobody any damn good.

I BIT INTO THE TACO THAT WAS IN FRONT OF me. My apartment felt tiny tonight. Abuelita had sent me home with tacos after I'd stopped in at my parents' after work, but there was something about tonight that felt hollow.

I knew what it was.

I spoke to Aspen every single day.

Today, I hadn't.

You could call it what the fuck you wanted, but it'd been radio silence since I'd kissed her yesterday.

She'd been radio silence for days, truth be told. We wouldn't have spoken if I hadn't gone to see her at work. We'd be stuck in a worse fucking limbo than we already were.

I pushed the taco away from me. I wasn't hungry. Honestly, I felt sick.

Why had I pushed it? Why had I pushed her into talking about it? She'd clearly forgotten that she'd admitted she remembered.

If I'd just left it. If I'd just shut my big fucking mouth. It would be fine.

I stood, grabbing the plate from the table and taking it into the kitchen. I tossed the leftover taco into the trash and dumped the plate in the sink. I didn't really know what to do with myself right now, so I just kind of stood there.

Until there was a knock at the door.

"Luke, let me in!" Blaire's voice crept through the cracks.

I dropped my head back. No. Blaire was the very last person I wanted to see right now. She was way too fucking bubbly for my mood.

"Go away," I yelled back at her.

"Open this door, or I'll kick it in!"

Sadly, I knew she wasn't lying. At the very least, she'd give it a good old fucking try until I ultimately opened it.

With a sigh, I went to the sofa. "It's open."

The door swung open, and Blaire marched in right as my ass hit the sofa. "You kissed her?" she demanded, standing by the door, clutching the handle.

I stared at her. "I kissed her."

"Thank fuck for that." She shoved the door shut and came over to me. "One of you had to do somethin'."

"You think it's a good thing?" I shook my head. "You're an idiot."

"Nah, you're the idiot. You're both idiots. It's like wrangling cats into a bath." She jumped onto the sofa and grabbed the open bag of chips from the table. "She's ignoring you. Did you know that?"

"No, really? I thought she'd gone on an expedition to the Arctic and that was why she hasn't spoken to me since."

"You don't need to be cocky with me, Luke. Believe it or not, I'm here to help you."

"Is that by eating all my food?"

"I hardly think a packet of chips constitutes as all your

good." She paused, hand deep in the bag. "Then again, this is you, so it probably is."

I snatched the bag from her and shoved my hand in it. "Fuck off."

"You either want my help or you don't."

"I don't remember asking for your help."

"Fine." She held up her hands and got up. "You figure out how to handle this by yourself."

"Woah, woah—I didn't say I didn't want it."

Blaire stopped, putting her hands on her hips and pinning me with a hard stare. "Okay, but you're going to listen to me, and you're not going to argue with me."

"Eesh. I don't know if I can do both of those things."

"Fine. You'll listen to me, but I will accept occasional, mild arguments."

I nodded. "That works. Sit down."

"All right." She pulled a hairband off her wrist, snapped it, and shoved her hair up into a ponytail before sitting down. "You need to speak to her. Now."

"I tried." I put the bag of chips onto the coffee table and brushed the crumbs off my fingers. "I called her this afternoon, but she sent it to voicemail."

"She was working this afternoon. They have a wedding party at the weekend, and Dec gave her tonight off if she'd go in and help him organize stuff."

"She at work now?"

Blaire shook her head.

"Then she could have called me." I shrugged. "There are only so many more times I can call or chase her down at work before someone thinks I'm a crazy stalker and I get arrested."

She leaned back, sighing. "She's too stubborn for her own good, but Luke? She's just afraid. She's embarrassed because of what happened, and she doesn't know what to say to you after what you said to her."

"I told her how I felt. I had to be honest with her. If we'd been honest with each other in the first place, we probably wouldn't even be in this situation."

"No, you probably would." Blaire paused when I glared at her. "What? You think the level of attraction you feel toward another person is based on honesty? If that were the case, we'd all be attracted to our moms."

"Nah, they lie. Santa. Tooth Fairy."

"All right, fine, we'd all be attracted to our palms and vibrators." Another pause. "Although…"

"Don't need to know about your vibrator," I said quickly. "Where are you going with this?"

"Okay." She tucked her feet under her butt and, with her elbow on the back of my sofa, propped up her head. "You need to just do it. Go to her place and pin her to the wall until she talks. If all else fails, you can fuck it out of her."

"I'm almost entirely certain I need her consent for that final part."

"Yeah, well, she'll give it. She told me how you kissed her. I'm pretty sure she described it as a fairytale."

I raised my eyebrows.

"So, you need to sweep into her apartment, grab hold of her, and demand she tells you the truth about how she feels."

"Jesus, Blaire, you watch too many movies." I got up and walked into the kitchen to get a beer.

"Yeah, except I don't want that romance shit. I prefer it when people die." She snorted, looking over her shoulder. "Did you know that Tom and I broke up six months ago?"

"You look pretty together to me," I said dryly.

"We are. It didn't last long. You know what he did when I told him to fuck off and stormed out of his apartment? He followed me to my car, then pushed me against it and kissed the hell out of me until I forgave him."

"Blaire, that's not a breakup. That's you having a bitch fit."

"I told him to die and go to hell."

"Again, that's you having a bitch fit."

"Not the point. The point is, he came after me. He wasn't willing to let me go."

"A severe lack in judgment, given that you'd just willed him to burn in hell."

She shrugged. "Still. Listen to me. He wanted me. He came after me. If you really want to change your situation with Aspen, sitting on your ass waiting for her stubborn one to come to you isn't going to change a thing. All it's going to do is make you lose her. You have to take control of this situation."

I took a long drink from my beer and leaned against the kitchen counter. I knew what she was saying. I knew, deep down, that she was right. I had to go after her again and sort this out for real, but it was hard.

I was afraid.

I didn't want to lose my best friend.

"Luke." Blaire got up and walked over to me, grabbing my upper arms. "I know you're scared, too. But what are you more scared of? Walking over there and finding out you're the only one who feels this way? Or are you afraid of losing her from your life forever?"

I didn't answer.

"All right." She stepped back and took a deep breath. "As both y'all's best friend, I did my job here." She held up her hands and grabbed her purse from the table. "I'll talk to you tomorrow."

She left with a wave, and I stared after her.

She was right.

I hated it when Blaire was right.

I put the bottle on the counter and stalked to the door

where my sneakers were. I shoved my feet into them and grabbed my keys from the side, barely pausing to lock the door behind me.

I ran down the stairs faster than I ever had in my life. My truck was only a few feet from the door, and I climbed in and started the engine before I'd even shut the door.

Two knocks sounded at my window.

I rolled it down.

Blaire had one eyebrow raised. "What are you doing?"

"If this goes wrong, I'm taking your ass down with me," I warned her, putting the truck into reverse.

She laughed, stepping clear of my path. "And we'll go down swinging. Totally okay with that."

I grinned at her, rolled the window back up, and backed out of the space, ready to go.

"Wait! I have an idea!" She ran back to me and pulled open the passenger side door. "She won't answer the door if she knows it's you."

"What about your car?"

"I walked. Her place is closer to mine than yours is. Think about it as you giving me half a ride home in exchange for me getting you into her apartment."

"I'm not climbing through a window."

"Nothing that dumb," Blaire said. "Although, I've climbed out of a couple after bad dates. But no, I'm going to knock and tell her it's me, then run."

"And leave me to face her wrath?"

"Hey, if this goes to plan, you could get laid by the end of the night."

"And if it goes wrong, I could be castrated."

"Orgasms can come at a price. Aspen's is gonna be expensive after the stunt you pulled." She tapped twice on the dash. "Let's go!"

I was regretting this already.

SIXTEEN

ASPEN

Ice-Cream Does Not Cure All

I STARED AT THE TUB OF BEN AND JERRY'S IN front of me.

They'd done me well, these two. They'd been my friends through countless periods, bad dates, and breakups.

But, tonight, today, they just weren't cutting it.

Apparently, there was no cure-all for having bad sex with your best friend, then getting drunk and admitting it, then him kissing you.

Not that I was surprised. That was a loaded situation.

I put the lid back on the tub and, with a sigh, got up to put it back in my freezer.

Knock knock.

"There's nobody home," I shouted, putting the tub

back on its spot on the shelf and shutting the freezer door.

"Yeah, that'll deter an ax murderer," Blaire shouted from the other side. "Let me in, Asp. I just came from Luke's."

"I don't want to talk about him."

"You don't have to. Promise."

I sighed again and unlocked the door, opening it.

That was not Blaire.

That was Luke.

I blinked at him.

"For the record," he said, holding up his hands. "Not my idea."

"I'm gonna kill her." I let go of the door and walked back inside. When he didn't move, I said, "Are you gonna come in or not? I figure you didn't come here to stand in the hallway all night."

Luke walked into my apartment and shut the door behind him. "We really have to talk about this."

"Want a drink?" I pulled the tequila bottle from the corner of the counter and grabbed a shot glass.

"Based on recent history, I'm going to go with no."

"Suit yourself." I poured a shot and tossed it back. "I figure it can't get much worse at this point."

"Aspen…"

I took a second shot and instantly regretted it. It burned. "No, look. Listen to me. We got drunk and had bad sex that, apparently, both of us remembered despite thinking otherwise—"

"Yeah, I'm pretty sure I still come off worse after that night."

"Then, I get dirty dreams about you because, apparently, you look really good naked, and my subconscious had a bet with my awake brain that you were better in bed than copious amounts of tequila led me to believe."

"I agree with your subconscious."

"Then, I get drunk and tell you I remember just how bad it was, how you were a pretty little tap-tap-squirt, but, Luke? Don't tell Luke!" I gripped the neck of the tequila bottle tightly. "Then, you show up at my work, tell me you want me, and kiss me like it's the end of a fucking Disney movie."

"Probably the best compliment I've had in a long time about my kissing."

"Luke!"

"What?" He threw his arms to the side. "What do you want me to say to you, Aspen? Ever since Sunday, you've been hiding and ignoring me. You want me to stand here and tell you I'm sorry I was honest with you? That I'm sorry I kissed you? Because I'm not, and I'm not. All I want to do is figure out what the fuck we do now, but I can't do that because you're hiding away like a child!"

My eyebrows shot up. "I'm not a child!"

"Then, for fuck's sake, act like it!" He ran his fingers through his hair. "You're my best friend. You think I like this situation? I don't, but I want to fix it."

I glared at him.

"Even now, standing in front of me, you can't talk to me. Why can't you just be honest?"

"Because," I said, dropping my eyes. "I'm afraid that being honest means losing you, one way or another."

"Now, we're getting somewhere." He leaned on the other side of the island, pressing his hands flat against the top of it. "Why?"

"Because you're my best friend," I replied softly, bringing my gaze up to meet his bright blue one. "And I don't see any way out of this situation where we go back to normal."

"There isn't a way," Luke said, his gaze never leaving mine. "There is no way we can go back to before we had sex, Aspen. Not unless one of us suddenly acquires a time machine. You got one of those?"

"If I did, we wouldn't be having this conversation." I put the cap back on the tequila bottle and replaced it on the other counter.

His lips tugged to one side, lighting his eyes up. "Same. We just can't ignore this. I know what I want to do, but I need you to tell me where you want to go from here."

I bit the inside of my lower lip, darting my gaze away from him.

Truth be told, I hadn't stopped thinking about kissing him since he'd kissed me. I wanted to do it again, but the implications of it terrified me.

We had an easy relationship. We took each other to family weddings. We hung out all the time. We bailed each other out of bad dates. Twenty years of being friends had put us in a status quo that was comfortable.

Kissing again would be a twist that I didn't know if we could unravel from.

"Well?"

I wrung my fingers in front of me. "I don't...want things to change," I said slowly and quietly. "But that doesn't mean it doesn't feel like it is changing."

"It is changing. I mean, three weeks ago you were still the little chubby-cheeked kid who I protected from boys."

I smiled.

"Now..." He sighed and dropped his chin.

Yup. That just about summed it up.

"Maybe it's just an itch." I bit my lip. "Maybe it's just curiosity on our part. I mean, what we really did wasn't sex. It didn't really have a satisfying conclusion."

"Not for you," he pointed out.

"Really? You think that was satisfying?"

He held his hands up. "Never mind. Carry on."

"Thank you." I crossed to the fridge and got a bottle of water. "It's a loose end. We didn't tie it up. Like... most times when you have sex, you're either in a relationship, or it's clearly a one-night-stand."

Slowly, Luke nodded. "It makes sense."

"Ours was a drunken hook-up that, honestly, barely even qualifies as that."

"What are you saying?"

What was I saying? Excellent question. I wasn't quite sure.

"I, um, I don't know." I shifted to the side a little. "But I think I'm saying we either draw a line under what happened or we...don't."

He quirked one eyebrow, his lips tugging up with it. "Are you suggesting we have sex?"

Boy, this was awkward.

"Maybe. A little bit." I grimaced and fiddled with the hem of my shirt. "Look, I think the way we feel is pure curiosity and the only way to stop this..." I waved between us. "Is to either say it'll never happen or just do it."

"Just do it, she says. As if you're going to clean a toilet."

"Well, sex does involve a bit of plunging. Like cleaning a toilet."

He pressed his hand against his forehead. "Please don't ever use the words 'sex' and 'plunging' in the same sentence ever again."

"I'm trying to make it a little less awkward."

"What? By comparing sex with cleaning a toilet? It isn't working, Asp. You're just making it weird."

"You brought up the toilet thing. Besides, this entire situation is weird. It can't get any weirder."

"Yes, it can."

"How?"

"By you comparing sex to cleaning a toilet!" He laughed, walking over to me. He pried the bottle of water from my fingers and cupped my face. His palms were rough against my cheeks, and his fingers teased my hair. "I know what I want, all right? I want to take you back into your room and prove to you I'm a lot more than tap-tap-squirt."

"I'm never going to live that phrase down, am I?"

"Yeah, well, I'm never gonna live down being the tap-tap-squirt, so we're about even here." His eyes sparkled. "But I'm not going to make you do anything you don't want to. I just want to be done with this awkwardness. It's up to you."

I groaned, leaning forward into him. Laughing, he wrapped his arms around my shoulders and held me tight.

Why'd he have to put it on me? Why couldn't he just make the choice for me? Being a grown-up sucked. When you were a kid, you didn't really have to take responsibility for bad decisions. It was just, 'Oh, she'll learn!'

Yeah, well, I fucking didn't.

I took a deep breath and stepped away from him. "Okay. Let's do it. Let's have sex."

His eyebrows shot up. "Are you sure?"

"Yes. Let's do it." I nodded. "I think."

"You think. That's not sure."

"Well, I think I'm sure. That's kind of sure."

"Aspen, if we have sex, and it turns out that it's not idle curiosity, that there's something else here, we can't turn back from that."

Shit. Shit. "I'm not sure."

"Okay, come here." He grabbed my hand and tugged me into him. "Let me help you with that."

Before I could ask how, he cupped the back of my neck and brought my lips to his. My heart did a happy flip, and my body reacted way before my brain did.

My brain was still stuck on the potential of there being more than curiosity when my hands clutched at his shirt.

Kissing him was easy. Weirdly so. His lips were soft and warm and full and tasted mildly of beer and tacos. On anyone else, that would have been a totally not-sexy combination, but on him...

I was losing my mind. Mostly because now I had my arms around his waist and his tongue was teasing at the seam of my mouth.

I let him in, bringing my body closer to his. His hand was splayed on my upper back, his other cupping my ass and pinning me to his solid abs.

Fireworks erupted across my skin. All I could feel was him and the way he kissed me, the way he held me so tight against him that I could feel how badly he wanted me.

His cock was solid and pressing against my stomach. The twinges of desire that I'd fought back rushed through me at the feeling of that, and I knew that we'd crossed the line.

There was no going back from here.

I pulled back from him. I was flushed, and my cheeks burned. My chin was tingling from where his stubble had brushed against me.

I said nothing.

I simply took his hand and pulled him into my room. The second we were through the door, I grabbed the collar of his t-shirt and kissed him again.

Luke's hands immediately went to my ass, tugging me right against him. We both staggered back toward the bed.

"Take your shoes off," I muttered against his lips. "And your socks. I'm not having sex with someone wearing socks."

He burst out laughing, sliding his hands up to my hips

and leaning back so he could look down at me. "You know, if I didn't feel the same way about socks during sex, I'd be annoyed you just interrupted us to say that."

I held up my finger and sat on the edge of the bed, then peeled off my socks. Waving them in front of him, I grinned, then tossed them to the side.

"So sexy." He rolled his eyes before kicking off his shoes and doing the same with his socks. "Happy now?"

"No. Take off your shirt."

"You're demanding."

"I get to be demanding."

Laughing again, he grabbed the bottom of his shirt and pulled it over his head, revealing his tanned, muscular body.

Seriously.

Was it sculpted? Shouldn't he be in a museum?

"Aspen? Can you stop staring? I've got eight inches of cock getting impatient."

My gaze dropped to his erection. "Really? Eight inches? Isn't the average, like, five?"

He smirked. "I'm above average."

"Yeah, well, we'll see about that pretty soon."

"Jesus, you talk a lot for a woman who just dragged me into her bedroom." He grabbed my hands and pulled me up off the bed.

"Yeah, well, I—"

He kissed me to shut me up. "Shut up and take off your shirt."

Before I could move, he grabbed the bottom of my tank top and pulled it up, forcing me to lift my arms so he could remove it.

"Now, for real—stop talking." He kissed me again, then pushed me back onto the bed. I squeaked as I landed on the mattress and bounced, but any protest was silenced by him leaning over me, slipping one leg between mine and covering my mouth with his.

My fingers drew patterns up and down his back as we kissed, and when he moved his mouth down the side of my neck, it felt like the most natural thing ever.

I let go of the weirdness of this being Luke, my best friend, and gave myself over to the moment.

It took him no time at all to make his way down my body and grab the waistband of my shorts. I was breathing short and sharp by this point, so I didn't question when he pulled them over my ankles and went back for my underwear.

Then, holy crap, I was naked, and his face was between my legs.

I gasped at the first contact between his tongue and my clit. It was like someone had lit a spark inside me, and by the time he'd fully parted my legs with his hands, I could hear the blood pumping inside my ears.

He took his time, wielding his tongue like a weapon, toying with me over and over. He knew exactly what he was doing, and I squirmed in delight as he slid one finger inside me, adjusting his head so he had room.

My hips bucked. My heart was going crazy against my ribs. I could barely control my breathing as he worked me up to the edge, adding more and more pressure with his tongue until I lost control.

I clawed at the sheets, arching my back as the pleasure rushed through me. I knew I was trembling. I was hot all over; I couldn't think. It was a hazy fog descending over my mind, and as I threw one arm over my eyes, I vaguely heard the opening and closing of a drawer and something swishing.

I was oblivious to everything until Luke leaned over me, slipping easily between my legs. He chuckled low, bringing his lips to mine. They tasted a little like me, but I still wrapped my legs around his hips to force him inside me.

My brain was mush, but my body was wide awake.

He reached down between us, his thumb brushing my clit as he did, and guided himself inside me. I was so wet it wasn't exactly hard, but he still took his time as he eased into me and my hips angled up.

He kissed me as he moved inside me, long, slow strokes that were both infuriating and sexy at the same time. His tongue battled mine in time with his thrusts, and as the first moan left my lips, I felt him smile.

Smug little bastard.

One of his hands trailed down my body, sliding right down over my thigh and back up. His touch was red-hot, and it wasn't long before I was victim to another orgasm as it built inside me. The faster Luke fucked me, the faster it came.

My nails were in his back as I gripped at him for dear life. I didn't want him to stop. I wanted—needed—him to keep going, keep moving, keep turning up the pressure before I went insane with waiting.

So, he did.

He sat up, gripping my hips, and fucked me even deeper that way. I knew his eyes were on me, blazing with desire, but I couldn't hold on any longer.

The orgasm came at me much like the first—slamming through me with an intense pleasure I'd rarely ever felt before.

Luke's groan cut through my own, and he thrust into me really hard, then stopped, loosening his grip on my ass to lean forward and rest his forehead on my shoulder.

We lay there like that for a minute, catching our breath, with him still inside me and me covering my eyes while I recovered.

"Thanks for maiming my shoulders," he breathed,

lifting his head slightly.

"You're welcome," I whispered back. "Thanks for turning out to be above average in bed."

He laughed, the sound thick and husky as he pressed his face into my neck. "Well, now you know I wasn't lying." He kissed the side of my neck and got up, slowly pulling out of me. "Do you want to shower first, or should I?"

SEVENTEEN
ASPEN

Grinches and Banshees… And A Morning After

I TIED THE BAND AROUND THE BOTTOM OF MY wet braid and shook my head from my perch on the kitchen island. I was sitting in the middle of it, legs crossed, surrounded by food.

"There's absolutely no way Voldemort would beat Harry."

Luke raised his eyebrow and grabbed a handful of fries. "How do you know?"

"There are literally seven books and eight movies about how Voldemort could not kill Harry Potter."

"All right, but if Harry wasn't the master of death…"

"Now, you're just clutching at straws." I shook my head again and grabbed a slice of pizza. "Your argument has no merit. Give up."

"I never give up. Not against you."

"I know. You're an idiot. You cannot win an argument against me." I tore a bite of pizza off. "Just face it."

"You're so hot, eating with your mouth full."

"I'd throw this pizza at you if I weren't dying of starvation."

He snorted, grabbing his own slice. "No, you wouldn't. I've never seen you throw food. Ever."

"Food is sacred. It should never touch the ground."

"It wouldn't. I'd catch it. I fully agree with you."

I bit into the last bit of the slice that had sauce and tossed the crust into the box. "Whatever. Voldemort could still never beat Harry. I don't care what you say, I'm right."

"Sure, you're right." He shrugged a shoulder and dipped some fries into the tub of ranch before shoving them in his mouth. "Always right. Except for my bedroom skills."

"You're so hot, eating with your mouth full," I shot back at him his own words. "And whose fault is it that I thought you had the skill of a virgin teenage boy? You were hardly pornstar of the year two weeks ago!"

He laughed, choking on the fries. He thumped his fist against his chest until he was able to speak again. "Pornstar of the year? I wouldn't go that far. Unless you had a secret video camera in there…"

I pointed at him. "I only let you in because I thought you were Blaire."

"You let me in all right."

Cheeks flaming hot, I blinked at him. "Your pun isn't funny."

"I thought it was." He grinned.

"No video camera." I redirected the conversation back around. "I said you were above average, don't get cocky."

"You just said I'm better than at least fifty percent of the male population. How can I not get cocky?"

"Because by that calculation, at least forty-eight percent of the population could potentially be better in bed than you."

He shook his head, tossing his own crust in the box. "Wow, Asp. You really know how to build a guy up."

I leaned back and raised my eyebrows. "I just came twice in fifteen minutes and scratched the crap out of your back. I don't think I need to feed your ego anymore."

"Egos always need feeding."

"So do internet trolls, but it doesn't mean you should serve them a three-course dinner."

"Point taken."

I grinned, uncrossing my legs and stretching them out. Luke grabbed more fries and dipped them again while I reached for the water I'd opened but not drank a while ago.

We sat in amicable silence for a few minutes before I said, "It's different now, isn't it?"

Luke slowly slid his gaze toward me. "Yeah. It's different."

I rested my feet on the stool next to him and toyed with the bottle. "It wasn't curiosity, was it?"

"Do you think it was?"

I looked at him. Really looked at him. His dark hair was a hot, scruffy mess on top of his head. His blue eyes were soft but curious, and the stubble that darkened his jaw was just long enough that it was begging me to run my fingers over it.

And... I shook my head.

"Me either," Luke said quietly.

"What do you want to do?"

"I don't know," he replied. "Do you?"

"Nope." I smacked the 'p.' "We maybe should have thought this through a little more before...you know."

"Before I fucked you into oblivion?"

"I didn't leave the bedroom, never mind making it far enough into orbit to get to oblivion. Calm yourself, Shrek." I laughed.

"Shrek? For fuck's sake. Not the sex face thing again." He shook his head.

"What?" I grinned, leaning forward and resting my arms on my knees. "It's true. Your sex face is a cross between Shrek and the Grinch, just not so green. But totally as hairy today." I reached out and tickled his chin.

He batted away my hand. "We're not discussing sex faces. You won't like what I have to say about yours."

"Why? What's wrong with my sex face?"

"Well... You look a little like a banshee."

"A banshee?" My voice rose several octaves. "A fucking banshee?"

His lips twitched as he fought his smile. "Yeah. You know, eyes wide, mouth in a big ol' 'o' shape..."

"A banshee?" I couldn't believe he was calling me a banshee. Or more specifically, my sex face.

"Why are you so offended? You called me a cross between Shrek and the Grinch!"

"Yeah, well—" I stopped. "You're unfairly handsome on a regular day, so it only fits that your sex face is super ugly."

He grinned. It was the kind of grin that reached his eyes and made them sparkle—and made my stomach flutter.

It was unsettling.

The fluttering—not the grin.

"You think I'm unfairly handsome?"

"Ugh." I slid off the island. "That was what you took from that? Couldn't you focus on the 'super ugly' part?"

"No. That doesn't do my ego any good. Why would I

focus on that?"

"Of course." I shook my head. "Why would you?"

He laughed and got up, wiping his fingers on a napkin. "It's getting late. I should probably head out. I have to work tomorrow."

I paused, turning around. "You don't—I mean, it's not like you've never stayed here before."

He quirked a brow. "Are you asking me to stay?"

"No." I bristled. "I'm saying you don't have to leave if you don't want to."

Luke walked over to me, stopping just a few inches in front of me. "If you want me to stay, just say it."

I folded my arms to put a little barrier between us. "I'm not saying that."

"So, you want me to leave?"

"Why are you so awkward? Stay or go. Your choice." I poked him in the chest. "But I am going to bed. I'm tired."

"Yeah?" His grin was lopsided. "Are you?"

I clicked my tongue and stalked toward my room. "Whatever. Do what you want."

"I'm coming with you. It won't be nearly as awkward when I wake up with an erection this time."

I shot him a look over my shoulder and grabbed a t-shirt and pair of shorts to wear to sleep in. "That is never not going to be awkward."

He shrugged and pulled his shirt back off. "Maybe for you."

Oy. Why had I opened my big mouth?

"REMEMBER HOW ABUELITA SAID I NEEDED TO marry a woman who can cook?"

I eyed Luke, pausing with my pancake on my spatula. "Tread very carefully."

"I think I might marry you," he said, grabbing the syrup bottle. "You're hot, good in bed, and you can cook. That's like the magic trifecta. Plus, we already know each other."

"That's not superficial at all." I slid my pancake onto my plate and joined him at the island.

"What? Looks, sex, and food. That's all a man needs in a wife."

"Wrong. He also needs her to have the patience of a saint if that's the kind of bullshit she has to listen to."

"Ah, shit, yeah." He paused. "Well, that puts you out of the running."

I flipped him the bird and shoved a slice of bacon into my mouth. Such an ass. Not that I knew how we'd gone from having sex to him deciding he was going to marry me.

Clearly, he was thinking with both his dick and his

stomach.

It wasn't a very intelligent combination.

"For that, you can make your own coffee," I said, getting up to go to the coffee machine.

"For what? The trifecta comment, or the part where I said you have no patience?"

"Both, you dick." I hit the button on the coffee machine. "And no, you can't use one of my to-go coffee cups just because you're late for work."

"Ah, look. Who needs to get married? We've been acting like it for years. It's good to know that blowing your mind hasn't changed your attitude toward me."

"Jesus, Luke, if I knew that having sex with you would turn you into a high school jerk, I'd have kept my legs shut."

He choked on his juice. "I forgot how nice you are on a morning."

Cradling my cup of coffee, I turned around, glaring at him over the rim.

"You're also very pretty on a morning."

"Stop sucking up to me." I hid my smile behind the cup. "It's not working."

He folded a pancake in two and tore off a bite. "Then why are you smiling?"

"Don't eat with your mouth full. It's gross."

"You did it last night."

"It's my apartment. I can do what I want." I poked my

tongue out at him and walked to the front door to answer the knock. I twisted the key and pulled it open.

Shit.

"You can fuck off," I said to Blaire. "Traitor."

"Yeah, yeah, whatever." She pushed me to the side, storming her way into my apartment.

I barely had to a chance to steady myself before she stopped.

A large grin broke out on her face when she saw Luke sitting at my island. "Let's see. Wet hair, yesterday's clothes, enough food to feed the five hundred... Hello, slut."

"'Sup," Luke said, nodding his head while reaching for another slice of bacon.

My cheeks flamed as Blaire's eyes met mine. I mouthed, "Not now," but said out loud, "Coffee?"

"Oh, so she gets coffee, but I don't?" Luke pointed his piece of bacon at me with an annoyed look on his face.

"Yes. She's not thinking with her dick and her stomach." I snatched the bacon from him and put it in my mouth.

"Sharing food?" Blaire asked, setting her purse on the floor. "How romantic."

"You know where the coffee machine is." I detoured back around to my stool at the island and sat down. "I don't have to take this shit from you two."

She stuck her middle finger up at me and walked over

to the machine. "I'll make you a coffee, Luke. You're clearly exhausted. Was it a long night?"

I glared daggers at her back.

"Nope. I was asleep by eleven-thirty," he replied. "I just like coffee with my bacon on a morning."

"You probably don't even have any bacon in your fridge," I muttered into my cup.

"Correct. I don't." He flashed me a grin. "That's why I stayed here last night. So you can feed me."

"Yeah," Blaire drawled, pulling a cup from the machine. "That's why you stayed."

I glared at her some more.

Luke drained his juice and stood up. "Don't worry about my coffee, Blaire. I've gotta go home and get changed before work. I'll grab a cup there."

He was smarter than I gave him credit for. He clearly saw I would be more comfortable sitting on a cactus than I was in this conversation.

"Leaving so soon?" My best friend's eyes sparkled as she turned around.

"She's going to punch someone if I don't, and since I'm not being an ass, I'd rather it were you." He grinned, grabbing his phone and keys off the island and turning to me. "I'll call you later?"

"Working," I said.

"All right, so I'll see you later?"

"Given your habit for showing up, you probably will."
I half-smiled. "See you later."

He winked, tugged my hair, and threw Blaire a wave as
he left. The door shut, and the sound of it closing against
the frame seemed to echo through my silent apartment.

Blaire said nothing for a good minute. She simply stood
there, leaning against the counter, cradling her coffee cup in
front of her so she could blow into it. She watched me like
a hawk.

A hawk who wanted to be punched in the face.

I chewed on my bacon, waiting for her to say the first
word. She usually did. The first and the last was her M.O.
That was why she was even worse to argue with than I was.

"So," she finally said after a few minutes of waiting.
"You banged him, huh?"

"We did an experiment," I replied. "We wanted to see
if we felt the way we did because the first...accident...was
so bad."

"Okay, one: it wasn't an accident. Two: You didn't do
an experiment. You banged him."

"It was an experiment! We slept together purely to see
if we wanted to do it just because we were curious or
because there was...something...there."

"And?"

"And what?"

"Is there something there?"

I paused. "I think so. Either that or the two orgasms were given to me by witchcraft."

"Two? Hold up." Blaire put down her cup. "He couldn't even get your motor running the first time, yet this time, you're coming like you have an orgasm button on your ass?"

I shrugged. "I don't know, but I'm not going to complain."

"Wise. You've probably moaned enough in the last twelve hours."

I spat my coffee all over the leftover pancakes while she laughed. "Whatever."

"What happens now?"

Shrugging again, I stood up and took the plate of pancakes to the trashcan. "We don't know."

"You don't know? Look, Asp, even I have a clear plan of action after I bang a guy. He's either a keeper or I'm out of there."

"Wow. I bet Tom's so glad you don't play fast and loose with your standards."

"Har-har-har," she drawled. "He's the lucky one who gets a piece of this regularly." At 'this,' she motioned down her body. "The only one."

"I'm so glad you clarified." I put all the dishes in the dishwasher and started it. "We just don't know. I don't think either of us were prepared for the fact we'd feel something other than idle curiosity."

Blaire nodded like she understood. "Yet, he stayed the night. Was it different?"

"Yep." I popped the 'p.' "Like, I wasn't just lying next to Luke. I was lying next to this really hot guy with abs that would make a bodybuilder weep, and I woke up with his arm around me. It felt weird."

"Good weird? Or bad weird?"

"Just…weird. It's still Luke, you know? But I'm starting to think the weirdness is all in my head. It doesn't feel wrong at all. In fact, I'm way too comfortable around him. It's so…seamless."

She tilted her head to the side, slowly pushing her hair behind her ear. "It's so easy that you're afraid it's too easy."

Wrapping my arms around my waist, I nodded. "Way too easy."

She sighed, then looked at me with a resigned look. "I get it. You know I'm not really the emotional kind—"

"No, really? I'm shocked."

"Shut up." She bit back a laugh. "But I felt the same when I started dating Tom, and we were just friends, and even then that was only because we were both friends with Luke. Hell, we weren't even dating. We were just screwing."

"I remember the ass phone calls."

"My bad." She even blushed. "It was too easy to go from that to dating to actually being together."

I hugged myself even tighter. "Why did you bring him here last night? Tricking me?"

"Tricking is a strong word," she replied slowly. "I wanted to help. I just—I know you, Asp. You were beating yourself up about it, and when you do that, you have a tendency to become an ostrich."

"An ostrich?"

"Yeah, you bury your head in the sand and hope the bullshit will pass you by."

I wanted to argue with that but... yeah, yeah. She was right.

"I went to his place, and he looked like I'd just run over his puppy." She raised a shoulder nonchalantly and pushed off the counter, moving toward me to put her mug in the dishwasher. "I just—you have something. You have to talk it all over. I can see that you feel something else for him."

"I don't know what I feel," I admitted. "I need to figure it out. I just... What if I lose him, Blaire? I'd rather feel something for him and never take it any further than risk losing my best friend for good."

"Aspen, honestly," she replied, meeting my eyes. "You just have to take a chance, if that's what you want to do."

"That's the problem. I don't know what I want to do. I don't even know if we can turn a friendship into a romantic relationship without ruining everything."

I expected some kind of smart-ass response, but I

didn't get it.

Instead, Blaire wrapped her arms around me and hugged me tightly.

Blaire didn't hug.

Ever. Not even puppies or little kids or her own family.

Resting my head on her shoulder, I closed my eyes, and it was only then that I felt the tears roll down my cheeks.

Damn it.

EIGHTEEN

LUKE

Dirty Dreams < Sex < Jealousy

I WALKED INTO THE BAR, MY EYES INSTANTLY sliding to the brunette behind it. Aspen was laughing at something a guy close to our age was saying to her, her honey-colored eyes alive with amusement and her smile wide.

The twinge of jealousy that twisted my stomach pissed me off.

I hated it. I didn't want to feel this. I hated that seeing her laugh at a strange guy made the hairs on the back of my neck stand up. I hated that this was even a fucking thing for me.

Usually, this site would have me walking up and introducing myself as her best friend. That, or I'd observe from a distance, making sure the guy wasn't a dick to her.

Now, I wanted to walk over there and drag him away from her by his collar.

Something I had no right to do.

Hell, despite my quips about marriage this morning, even if she were my wife, I wouldn't have the right from stopping her from talking to someone. Especially not at work.

But I wanted to rip his ears right off the sides of his head.

Then, I wanted to choke him on them.

"You all right, man?" Will slapped me on the shoulder. "You look like you're plottin' a murder."

I rolled my shoulder and followed him up to the bar. "Not today. Maybe tomorrow."

His eyes followed mine. The guy was now leaning forward on the bar, and the sleeves of his t-shirt were rolled up a little higher than they had been before I'd looked a minute ago.

How did I know?

I'd rolled my sleeves up more than once to impress someone.

"Ah," Will said. "A guy hitting on Aspen."

"Not just a guy hitting on Aspen," Tom said, coming up next to me. "A guy hitting on the woman he slept with last night."

Will jerked away. "What?"

"I'm gonna fuckin' kill Blaire," I muttered, pushing away from both of them toward the bar. I smelled like sawdust and sweat with a little sea air mixed in from the build we'd been working on just a few feet from the beach, but it was probably better than anything that pretty boy she was talking to smelled like.

Fuck.

This was getting worse.

"You slept with Aspen?" Will hissed in my ear, grabbing my arm.

"It's a long story, but yeah," I replied. I reached up behind me and grabbed the back of my neck, dipping my head forward so I didn't have to watch the asshole at the end of the bar flirting with her.

Fuck, this was so different.

Where the hell had this come from? Not from having sex with her. This was more than me just being protective of her—this was me wanting to protect her. Hide her away from fucktards who just wanted to have sex with her and discard her.

Because fuck what I'd told her last night, it hadn't been curiosity for me.

I knew I wanted her. I knew I wanted more. I didn't know when it'd happened, and I didn't know why, and I couldn't put my finger on anything at all.

I just knew that I wanted Aspen Camden more than I'd

ever wanted anyone in my life.

I wanted my best friend more than I'd ever wanted another woman.

"Shit," Tom muttered, leaning forward next to me. His elbow nudged mine.

"He gave her his number on the back of his receipt," Will continued.

I ran my fingers through my hair.

"Houston, we have a problem," Tom continued, still muttering like a fucking five-year-old trying to get out of eating all the cookies.

"Houston, I need a spacewalk. Bring my beer outside, would ya?" I pushed off the bar and turned on my heel, walking to the front door.

The hot, late-afternoon air slammed into me the second I left the air-conditioned bliss of the bar. There were two tables on the patio outside, and I could see the beach from my new perch at the end of one of them.

What the fuck was wrong with me?

I bent over, resting my elbows on my knees, and buried my head in my hands. My fingers slid into my hair, and I dropped my chin so far it all but touched my chest.

What the hell was happening? What was this?

I wasn't the kind of guy who went insane over a woman just because we'd had sex. Aside from my cousins, Aspen and Blaire were the only two I'd ever actively protected, even if that had meant getting my ass thrown out of a bar because someone had pissed me off a little too much.

That had happened. Once or twice. Maybe three times.

All right, so there were three bars in the next town over I was no longer welcome in. But all I ever did was protect them from handsy little fuckboys.

The guy in the bar hitting on Aspen and making her laugh—he wasn't being a dick. I'd seen guys hit on her a thousand times. It wasn't a new thing. I was no rookie in being the guy best friend.

I knew my role.

Sit back. Bite my tongue. Drag the guy away when he got too much. Maybe throw him a right hook if he got a little cocky with me.

This—this was not my role.

Sitting outside the fucking bar, my head in my hands, feeling sorry for myself, was not what I did.

Not over Blaire. Not over any woman.

Not over Aspen.

But here I was.

Sitting outside, head in my hands, feeling sorry for myself. Over a guy hitting on Aspen.

Fuck me sideways and call me daddy. I was screwed.

"Here." Tom put a bottle down on the table next to me. "Drink that."

I did. Most of it, anyway. My lips formed a seal around

the top of the bottle that popped when I pulled it away. "Thanks."

Will met my eyes from the opposite table. "She threw his number away."

"What?" I jerked my head up.

"Yep. She smiled until he finally turned away. She swept that piece of paper under the bar and tossed it in the trash as she came to us."

A sick kind of satisfaction flooded through me, even though I had little reason to believe it was because of me. We hadn't exactly discussed what we were doing with our weird situation, but that didn't mean I didn't like what I'd heard.

Fuck, I loved it.

Screw you, pretty boy.

Not that I wasn't one.

No, fuck that, I wasn't. I was not a pretty boy who spent hours on my hair or who wore pants tighter than my girl's.

Not that I had a girl.

Nope. Not me.

I grabbed the beer and took a long drink. Fuck this shit. She wasn't mine. She was my best friend, but that was it right now. No matter how much I wanted to take the guy's number out of her hand and shove it up his nostril…

At this point, she was still just Aspen.

My best friend.

The girl I'd slept with last night.

The girl who was sending me mixed messages because she was just as lost as I was about this.

She was fucking Aspen, goddamn it.

She was not just Aspen.

She was Aspen.

Aspen.

"All right, Dec's given me ten minutes to sit with y'all, so shift over, I'm comin' through." Aspen scooted over to our table and set down a tray full of beer and chips and salsa. "The queso and sour cream are coming right out. Mostly because I reminded him that if he didn't give me them in ten minutes, he owed me another five."

She stepped up onto the bench next to me and perched on the table. Her thigh brushed against my upper arm.

Her skirt was skin-tight and, while sitting down, barely reached her knees. It hugged her figure like it was made for it. The white tank she had tucked into the skirt was just as tight and form-fitting, and fuck, did it show off her tits.

When did I notice this?

Shit.

Aspen ran her ponytail through her fist, pausing to tease out a knot. "How's work going?"

"Great," Tom replied. "Luke hasn't been catcalled for an entire three days."

Her lips pulled to the side into a smirk. "The women y'all've been whistling at have great taste," she said. "How many flipped you off?"

"All of them," Will admitted. "Except the one who waved at Luke."

Aspen's gaze slid to me, darkening as they did. "Color me surprised," she said. "I'd love to hang with y'all, but my break is over." She slid off the bench, wiping her hands over her ass.

"That's the fastest ten minutes ever," Tom said.

"Yeah, well, time flies when you're having fun." She smiled tightly and turned to walk back into the bar.

"That wasn't awkward at all," Will said, watching her go. "So, you gonna tell us how you ended up having sex with her?"

"No." I pulled my beer toward me and swigged from the bottle.

Tom raised his eyebrows. "You know Blaire already told me."

"You tell the story then."

"Or not," he finished.

I rubbed my forehead and rested my arms on the table. This whole situation was weird. I was feeling jealous over a guy giving her his number, and she disappeared the second Will said someone had waved at me.

And nobody had. The asshole was trying to get under

her skin, and it'd worked.

It was tough enough without anyone else getting involved.

Aspen reappeared with two small bowls of queso and guacamole. She put them down on the table without a word and walked back inside.

"Be right back." I pushed my bottle away and got up, following after her. The bar was freezing compared to outside, and I shivered as I approached the bar.

Aspen was standing at the other end, handing the same guy who'd slipped her his number another beer.

"Got a minute?" I interjected into the conversation.

Her eyes flickered between him and me. "Can you give me a second?"

"Nah, you're good, darlin.' Put it on a tab for me." The guy shot her the kind of smile you shoot the girl you want to fuck and dump the next morning. He left us alone, shooting me a dark look as he left.

I'm pretty sure the one I shot him was even darker.

"What's up?" Aspen asked me, a fake brightness in her voice.

I turned my attention back to her. "You ignoring me again?"

"Why would you say that?"

"Well, for a start, you haven't said a word to me," I said, resting my arms on the bar and leaning forward. "And as soon as Will said that a woman had waved at me, you left."

She raised one eyebrow, grabbing a glass and wiping out the inside of it with a cloth. "Coming from the guy who saw me talking to another guy and walked out to sit outside."

"Not the point."

"Totally the point. You're allowed to be jealous, but I have to like it that a random woman waves at you?"

"I'm not jealous," I lied. "I just don't like the look of the guy."

"Mhmm."

"And you weren't just talking. I saw him give you his number."

"Which I promptly dropped in the trash," she replied smartly, putting down both the glass and the cloth. She gripped the edge of the bar and fixed me with a look that said she saw right through me. "Does that make you feel better?"

Yes.

"There's nothing to feel better about. I'm not jealous." I shrugged. "I just wanted to know if you were okay, that's all."

"I'm fine. Better?"

"Sure." Pausing, I glanced over my shoulder at the guy who was watching us. "You really threw out his number?"

She jerked one shoulder. "I didn't want it. He just kind

of shoved it at me."

"Really?"

"Yeah. Why does it matter, Mr. Not Jealous?"

"It doesn't matter. But, you know, just in case it did…" I leaned over the bar, cupped the back of her neck, and kissed her.

Her cheeks flushed when I pulled back. "Yeah. Not jealous my ass."

I grinned, chucked her under the chin, and headed back outside to the guys.

"A LITTLE BIRDIE TOLD ME YOU KISSED ASPEN yesterday." Mom slid a sandwich across the table to me. She had one eyebrow raised, and she was looking at me the way she did when I was a kid and she knew I was lying about something.

It was her, "Tell me everything and I won't get your grandmother with her flip-flop" look.

It worked every time.

"I did." I took the glass of Pepsi she offered me and sipped.

"Well? Is that all you're going to say? You kiss your childhood best friend and that's it?"

"Who kissed who?" Abuelita demanded in Spanish, shuffling through to the kitchen in today's bright outfit: a purple skirt with a green t-shirt and a yellow sweater.

Mom glanced at me with an evil glint in her eye. "Luke kissed Aspen."

Abuelita stopped. She brought her wrinkled hands to her cheeks, her mouth dropping open. "You kissed Aspen?"

I knew coming here today was a bad idea. "I kissed Aspen," I confirmed.

"Are you getting married?"

Whoa.

"We just kissed, Abuelita. We're not getting married." I bit into my sandwich.

She rushed over to me and took my hands in hers, almost making me drop my sandwich. "This is wonderful!" She continued on in Spanish, telling me in no uncertain terms that I had to marry Aspen, have beautiful little babies, and buy a house and get a Labrador.

"Whoa, whoa, Abuelita," I said, ignoring Mom's giggling from the sink. "We just kissed. Don't plan out our future yet. We haven't even had a chance to talk properly."

"You two might not have, but you're the talk of the town," Mom added. "I found out at the post office this morning."

"Really? People are talking about one kiss?"

"Why? Have there been more?"

"Do you really want me to answer that?"

She paused. "The nosy person inside says yes, but as your mother, no." She shook her head. "But yes, people are talking about it. Come on, Luke. You've been best friends since the day you started school, but then you lean over the bar and kiss her like you're dating her? People are going to talk."

"I knew I should have moved to Austin after high school. Nobody there would care if I kissed her."

"Everyone here would still know. Don't forget that Luisa is at college there."

I needed a smaller family.

"So you aren't marrying her?" Abuelita asked, finally letting go of my hands.

"Not in the plans right now," I replied. "But I'll let you know if that changes."

The theme tune to Wheel of Fortune came from the living room, and that was thankfully enough to make my grandmother shuffle out of the kitchen and stop marrying me off to Aspen.

I blew out a long breath and reached for my drink.

"I don't know if she's happy you might be seeing Aspen, or that Aspen is finally interested in one of her grandsons." Mom sat down opposite me.

"Definitely the last thing," I replied. "The last thing we

need is the entire town gossiping about us when we don't even know what we're doing."

"You should have thought about that before you kissed her in public."

She had a point. "Yeah, well, I wasn't thinking about that. I was thinking that the jerk who was hitting on her needed to back off."

Mom laughed. "Aw, my little boy—all jealous."

"Not jealous," I replied. "And I haven't been your little boy since I was eight and was actually smaller than you."

She leaned over and pinched my arm. "Don't sass me. You were jealous. You're allowed to be jealous, Luke. You care about her."

"Yeah, but I'm used to caring about her as her best friend. Not like this. I don't know how to handle these emotions where she's concerned."

"Roll with the punches. You don't have a choice. If you both feel the same, which I'm assuming you do, then you have to learn how to navigate your changing relationship together."

"I know that, but it's the learning part that's hard." I picked a slice of tomato out of my sandwich. "We've had a status quo for so long. We know the boundaries of our friendship, but now they've been crossed." Epically fucking crossed. "I don't know how to be anything but her best friend."

Mom sipped her Pepsi. "You can still be her best friend. That doesn't have to change just because your emotions have."

"That doesn't help."

"Do something different." She clasped her hands in front of her. "Do something together that you wouldn't do as friends. Treat your changing relationship as you should. If you were starting to date a stranger, would you lie around on the sofa, watching movies in your sweatpants?"

"Sounds like the perfect first date, if you ask me, but I think I see where you're going with this."

Her lips pulled up to one side. "Exactly. You'd do that later when you'd formed a friendship with them. You and Aspen already have that friendship, so that means you need to step out of your comfort zones. Take her out on a date. Don't take it for granted that you can make something romantic work just because you know each other inside out."

"I'm not. I think it's going to be harder than anything to make a romantic relationship work with her because if anything goes wrong, we'll never be able to get our friendship back to how it was."

"Sometimes that's a risk you have to take," Mom continued, her eyes gentle. "You can always turn back now. You don't have to take it any further than you already have."

Easy to say when she didn't know just how far we'd

taken it.

"But, if you really want to take a chance that you could make it work, you have to be ready to put in the effort. Think about it this way." She rested her hand on my arm. "You don't need to impress Aspen. She already knows all the good and bad parts of you, and if she can put up with you for twenty years, she's probably the kind of girl you really do need to marry, Luke. Not many others are going to cope with your crap."

I smiled. "Thanks, Mom. You know how to make a guy feel good."

"She's right!" Abuelita yelled from the living room. "Did you go shopping, or do I need to cook for you again?"

Mom might have had a point…

ME: I have an idea.

ASPEN: …Don't think too hard. You might hurt yourself.

She was a regular old comedian, wasn't she? I shook my head and tapped to open the keyboard again on my phone.

ME: I spoke to Mom earlier. She suggested we go on a date.

ASPEN: That's not you having an idea. That's you stealing your mom's.

ME: Semantics.

ASPEN: Important semantics. Are you asking me on a date, or is your mom doing it for you? Kind of like how Abuelita cooks for you.

ME: She cooks for you, too.

ASPEN: I know. I'm eating her food right now. By the way, did you know that you kissing me at work is basically the talk of the entire town? Thanks for that.

ME: I did know. How do you think my mom found out?

ASPEN: Does that mean Abuelita knows?

ME: Yes. She's already planning our wedding. She's ecstatic you're finally interested in one of her grandsons.

ME: Although, she did seem a bit put out that it's the one she's never tried to set you up with. She thinks she's losing her touch as a matchmaker.

ASPEN: She never had a touch as a matchmaker. Did she?

ME: No, but do YOU want to be the one to tell her that?

ASPEN: No. She'd cut me off. I need more quesadilla.

ME: You ate them all already?

ASPEN: Are you judging me? Cuz I already get that from my jeans. I don't need it from you, too.

ME: Your jeans judge you?

ASPEN: THEY SHOULD MAKE THE WAISTBANDS STRETCHY OKAY

ASPEN: YOGA PANTS DON'T JUDGE ME

ME: I'd be okay with it if you wore yoga pants all the time.

ASPEN: You and most other red-blooded men. I work hard for my ass.

ME: I don't want to hear about any other men.

ASPEN: Oooh. Are you getting jealous again?

ME: I wasn't jealous in the first place.

ASPEN: You're so full of shit there are aliens in another galaxy who can smell it.

ME: Smells like cotton candy.

ASPEN: No. I've used the bathroom after you. It does not.

I laughed. She wasn't wrong.

ASPEN: You said something about a date?

I took a deep breath. It'd seemed like a good idea before we'd gotten sidetracked, but now, I just felt nervous. I knew Mom was right—if we were going to date, we needed to act like it. We needed to push through the awkwardness to see if we really could be more than friends.

And the more I thought about it, the more I wanted to be.

Fuck, I wanted to be. I didn't want to think about her being with anyone else.

ME: Go to dinner with me? I'll book a table.

ASPEN: Holy crap, you really meant a date-date.

ME: I wasn't talking about the fruit.

ASPEN: We're really doing this?

ME: Mom suggested we step outside our comfort zone. It's not like we have to get to know each other, but if we lounge around at your place watching movies, that's not really a date. We do that every weekend.

ASPEN: And we've never been to dinner, so that's a logical step.

ME: Exactly. Are you in? Friday night?

ASPEN: Are you picking me up? Do I have to dress up?

ME: Yes, and yes. You wouldn't wear yoga pants on a first date, would you?

ASPEN: If I could get away with it, you bet your ass I would.

ME: You can't. Don't.

ASPEN: Fine. But you should know, I'm not putting out until the third date.

ME: That only works if you haven't already put out.

ASPEN: I'll put out if you pay. And if it isn't totally weird.

ME: Ah. I might eat all your food, but I am a gentleman. You can pay for date two.

ASPEN: Okay, but I'm wearing yoga pants on that one.

I grinned.

I was fine with that.

NINETEEN

ASPEN

How To Date Your Best Friend

I PACED BACK AND FORTH THROUGH MY living room, clothes strung over the back of the sofa. I was wearing nothing but a t-shirt and my panties, and Blaire was flicking through a magazine like I wasn't losing my mind over here.

"You have got to help me!"

Sighing, she put down the magazine and looked over at me. "You've been freaking out for hours. I don't know what to tell you. But I'm sure as hell not reminding you of his name since you already bit my head off once."

I groaned and sat down on the sofa, burying my head in my hands. "This is insanity, Blaire. What am I doing?"

"Yeah, this is the insane bit. You fucked your best friend, but going for dinner with him? Shock horror!"

I tossed a cushion at her. "I know that, but it's like… This is a date. A real date. We're actually going to be on a date."

"Say it again. I didn't understand that it's a date."

I pressed my face into my hands. "Don't. This changes everything, Blaire. Everything."

"So cancel it."

"I can't!"

"Why not?"

"I just can't." I paused, slumping back on the sofa.

She closed the magazine with a sigh and slid it onto the coffee table. "Do you have feelings for Luke?"

I did. I didn't know when they'd shown up, but they had. Yesterday, at work, when Will had said that some random woman had waved at him, a hint of jealousy had tickled across my skin. It'd been unsettling.

I was still unsettled.

If tonight went well—and it would, because it always did when we were together—it would mean we were officially dating.

It was one thing to have feelings for your best friend.

It was another thing entirely to date him.

I hadn't even come to terms with having feelings for him, never mind dating him. The whole situation was still weird to me.

It didn't matter that I'd liked it that he'd kissed me in

the bar yesterday. In front of all the people. Especially the guy who'd given me his number even when I'd said no.

Jealous Luke was a cute Luke.

It was even cuter that he denied being jealous.

"Aspen, listen. You'd feel like this no matter who you were going out with. Remember that guy you met on Tinder? You were practically shitting your pants before that date. What you're feeling is totally normal." Blaire met my eyes. "If you're really weirded out by it, don't take how you feel any further."

"I want to," I said softly, stopping fidgeting for the first time in ages. "But he's—"

"Your best friend. I know. But dating each other doesn't mean he can't still be that. Tom's pretty much my best friend outside you and Luke."

"But you dated first. The closeness of your friendship came after."

"So? Pretend you aren't best friends. It's stupid, but if you strip your relationship back down to basics, you'll probably find it's easier than you think."

That wasn't a bad idea. As dumb as it felt to pretend that we didn't know each other, it would remove that element of our relationship that we relied on so heavily.

It was ironic. The thing we were most comfortable with in our relationship was the thing making us so uncomfortable moving forward.

"We could do that," I said slowly. "That would make it feel more like a real first date and not two best friends playing relationships."

"See? I'm not just a pretty face. I have good ideas, too." She got up off the sofa. "Now, let's find a dress that will simultaneously knock his socks off and get his cock hard."

"Ah, the magic combination for a first date. A guy with an erection and no socks." I grabbed a red dress from next to me. "Actually, that's pretty much how my last first date went."

"Yes, but at least this time, you know you won't be accidentally having dinner with a nineteen-year-old student pretending to be twenty-five."

Score one for dating your best friend.

I WAS GOING TO THROW UP. I WAS SO CERTAIN of that fact that I'd put money on it.

No doubt about it. I'd never felt my stomach roll like this before a date. Not ever. It felt unnatural. In fact, if it weren't for the fact that my makeup was perfect, I'd probably run to the bathroom pre-emptively.

I wiggled my toes inside my shoes—not an easy thing

in heels—and stared at my front door.

He was late.

Why was he late?

Had he changed his mind? Had he decided that dating his best friend was too much after all? I wouldn't blame him. We could go back to normal.

Let's face it. If we dated, I'd have to feed him on a semi-regular basis, and I did that anyway. He stayed over. We'd even had bad, drunk sex.

We'd basically been dating for years, just without the physical or emotional side.

Just, you know. If we went back to normal, I'd probably compare every guy to him and use his kiss as the top level for kissing. I'd never date again because there was no way anyone could compare to him.

He'd move on easily. Look at him. He was perfection in a slightly lazy package. He'd get married to someone who would feed him and who his grandmother would love and he'd forget all about me.

Oh, Jesus, he'd forget about me.

That was why he was late.

He'd changed his mind and he was already forgetting about me.

I needed a drink.

I moved as quickly as my shoes allowed me to over to the corner where the tequila bottle was. Thirty seconds later,

I had the tiny glass full of liquid in my hand and was throwing it back like it was a magic potion that could cure all my problems.

Ironic, considering it was the root cause of all my current problems.

Three knocks thundered against my door, and I almost dropped the shot glass in shock.

"Uh—uh, hold on!" I shouted, shoving the dirty glass back into the cupboard and sliding the bottle back into the corner. It clinked against the vodka, and I winced, then quickly breathed into my palm to sniff my breath.

Tequila.

"Aspen? Are you okay?" Luke called through the door.

"Yeah! Just a sex! I mean sec—shit." I yanked open the medicine drawer and popped out two Gaviscon pills. I had no mints and no time to brush my teeth, so these would have to do.

I chewed like my life depended on it and, when I'd swallowed the last, chalky bit of mush, went to the front door. But not before I did another quick breath test.

Eh. Gaviscon, but better than before.

I pulled the door open and froze.

Luke's shirt looked starkly white against his tanned skin, and if possible, it made him even more handsome. It was tucked into perfectly-pressed black pants that rested upon shiny, black shoes. His dark hair was swept to the side, and his blue eyes shone brightly as they looked me up and down.

And, I'm not gonna lie, my heart felt as though it'd jumped into my throat at the sight of him.

"Hi," he said, bringing his gaze up to meet mine with the twist of his lips.

"Hi," I whispered, my own lips twitching into a tiny smile.

"You look beautiful." He took a step toward me, smiling a little wider.

"Thank you." I dipped my head, smiling. "You don't look so bad yourself."

He reached out and cupped my chin, tilting my head up. "You ready to go?"

I nodded.

"Hold on." He leaned in and softly kissed me, brushing his lips over mine and making my stomach flip. "Is that...Gaviscon?"

"Umm." I put on my sweetest smile. "Yes."

"I really shouldn't be surprised, should I?"

"Nobody wants trapped gas on their first date." I shrugged, taking a step back and grabbing my purse. "Should we go?"

Laughing, he stepped back into the hall so I could

lock the door, then took my hand with a wink. "Let's go."

I PEERED AT LUKE OVER THE TOP OF THE menu.

We'd had more than a few people stare at us when we'd walked into the restaurant. That was the problem with Port Wynne. There was only one fancy restaurant in the whole town, so we had no escape unless we left town, and we'd both agreed that was too much effort when we both lived right here.

"People are staring at us," I whispered into the crease of the menu.

"It's because they saw your ass in that dress as you walked in." He met my eyes. His were twinkling with laughter. "Don't worry about it. It's not like it's a secret there's something going on with us. I got stopped at the grocery store earlier by Lorna Raleigh and—"

"Wait, what?"

"I got stopped at the grocery store by Lorna Raleigh who asked me about us."

"I'm hung up on the fact you were at the grocery store." I put the menu down. "Are you kidding?"

He slowly shook his head. "See, it started when I went to get a snack after work, and I realized that if my date decided to go home with me tonight, I had nothing to feed her."

"Not even Abuelita's cooking?"

"No. I, er, ate it all."

"Are y'all ready to order?" Our server interrupted our conversation, looking directly at Luke even though she'd directed the question at us both.

Luke nodded, not even looking at her. "Are you ready?"

"Yeah. I'll have the shrimp tagliatelle, please." I folded the menu.

Luke placed his order and handed the server both of our menus. She shot him a stunning grin as she took them from him and spun on her heels.

I sipped my wine, glaring a hole in her back.

Luke picked up his glass, smirking. "What's up, Asp? You jealous?"

I jerked my head around so our eyes met. "No."

"If looks could kill, she'd be six foot under right now."

"I'm not jealous," I said firmly. "I just think she was a little too flirtatious for a girl at work. She's supposed to be professional."

He scratched his top lip, his hand hiding his smile. "You flirt with people all the time at work."

I gasped. "I do not!"

"You do. I've seen you pull your shirt down a little bit to get people to buy more drinks, and you do this girly little hair flip whenever you're talking to someone who's clearly attracted to you."

"Now who's jealous?"

"You. Because you won't be flirting with anyone anymore, or I'll kiss you even harder in public."

My eyebrows shot up. "It's my job to flirt with people."

"Aspen, you're a bartender. Not a hooker."

I ran my tongue over my lower lip. "You're right. I'm so in the wrong profession."

His eyes darkened, but he took a sip of his wine instead of talking straight away. "By the way, you just contradicted yourself. You said you didn't flirt, then said you did. Which one is it?"

"I'm friendly," I said quickly. "That's all. I have to be nice to people, even when I don't like them."

"That's why you and Blaire get along so well. You bond over your mutual hatred of most people."

"No." I tilted my glass toward him. "We bond over our mutual hatred of Justin."

He choked on his drink, putting the glass down. "By the way, he asked me today what I'd do if he asked you for your number again."

"What did you say?"

"I told him I'd shove him into a cement mixer and feed him to some chickens if he even thought about it."

I tilted my head to the side. "I thought you weren't jealous."

"I'm not. I've been telling him something similar for years. I just accompanied it with a punch this time." He grinned. "What? We're dating now. I get to do that."

"I don't think we agreed to dating. We're on a date. Dating would imply more than one."

"We can count the other as our first date."

"Right, if you counted sex as a first date, Blaire would be a serial dater."

"Instead of a serial slut?"

"I'd tell you not to call her that, but I'm pretty sure that's her email address for the dating websites she used to be on."

"Ah." Luke nodded. "That explains the numerous 'first dates' until Tom."

I laughed, propping my chin up on my hand. "No. I think Tom was like lightning for her. She had a crush on him the moment she laid eyes on him."

"I didn't know she was capable of human emotion."

"She is capable of surprising people every now and then."

He laughed, sitting back in his chair. "We can talk about her anytime. Let's talk about something different."

I raised my eyebrows. "Something different?"

"Yeah. This is about us pushing our boundaries of friendship, so… Let's do that."

"Okay, um." I spun my wine glass by the stem. "Any ideas?"

"Nope. None." He clicked his tongue a few times. "You?"

"Well, Blaire had an idea."

"Oh, God."

I dipped my head to hide my laugh. "It's actually not that bad. She suggested that we pretend this is a first date where we don't know each other the way we do."

Luke frowned. "You mean we go back to basics and tell each other about ourselves?"

"I guess, yeah."

"But we already know everything about each other. I know you can't use hair ties with the little metal clasp because your hair is too thick. I know you can't stand pantyhose because they never make them for long legs and the crotch constantly falls down. I know you can't stand to have the TV volume over fifteen, twenty if it's music, because it's just too loud for you to be able to concentrate."

A shiver danced over my arms.

Twenty years was a long time to be friends with someone, but it wasn't until it was in front of you that you realized just how well you knew a person.

"You know all those things?" I said softly. "Even the hair tie thing?"

"Yeah. You say it catches on your hair and those ties always break because the metal clasp is weak." He shrugged a shoulder. "I just—I've heard you complain about it so many times I never thought it would be something that would amaze you."

"I guess I don't think about it like that. It's just something that is for me. It's not something I ever thought you would have retained."

"Why? Because I forgot your birthday one year? I told you, I got my dates mixed up."

"No!" I covered my mouth while I laughed. "I forgave you for that when you showed up the next day with pizza, wine, and ice-cream."

"We're practically already dating. That's exactly how I'd show up if I was your boyfriend and we fought."

"No. If you were my boyfriend, you'd have to bring chocolate, candy, and chips on top of that. You'd also have to grovel for at least a week and tell me how pretty I am on an hourly basis."

"I'm starting to see why you've been single for a few years."

"No. I've been single for a few years because the internet is full of fuckboys, and Port Wynne is full of, well,

Justin."

Luke burst out laughing. "I can't comment on the fuckboys, but I'm there with you on Justin."

"Also, you're still single because you never go to the grocery store."

"Ah—I went today."

"Only because you're potentially getting laid."

His grin was lopsided. "Potentially?"

I pursed my lips at him, but hiding my smile was hard. "Yes, potentially. Would you have gone to the store if we weren't having dinner tonight?"

"No," he said quickly. "I'd have come to your place and eaten your food instead."

I stared flatly at him.

"See? Practically dating."

I reached for the bottle of wine to top up my glass, once again having to fight my smile as he grinned at me sexily. Thankfully, I was saved from replying by Flirty McFlirterson bringing our food over.

Pulling out her magic trick from when she took our order, she asked us if we needed anything else with her attention fully focused on Luke.

She didn't even look at me when he asked if I did.

I gave her back another deadly look as she walked away, ignoring Luke's breathy chuckling.

"Yeah. You're not jealous."

"I'm not jealous," I muttered. "I simply like to stare bitches to death."

"You should put that on a t-shirt. That'll scare them off."

I rolled my eyes and picked up my fork. "You're ridiculous."

He grinned again. Damn that grin. Why had I never noticed how sexy it was? What magic was this?

"All right. Let's do your thing while we eat."

"What thing?"

"The thing where we pretend we don't know a lot about each other. I think it could be fun. Like, I didn't know you had a jealous streak." His eyes shone with laughter.

I jabbed my fork into a shrimp. "I didn't know you had a jealous streak."

"I don't, but we're understanding now."

I sighed, putting the shrimp into my mouth and chewing. "Okay, fine." I set the fork down. "I work at Salty's Bar just a couple of blocks away from the beach. I have a borderline unhealthy relationship with Netflix and like quirky socks, and I can get a little wild after a few too many drinks."

Luke chewed, nodding his head. "Okay. Well, I'm a builder with Wynne and Sons with some of my friends. I once flashed the members of the bingo club in the town square after one too many tequila shots, and I am terrible at grocery shopping, so my grandmother often cooks me meals in batches." He paused. "Wait, scrap that last bit. That's not attractive at all."

"Not a good idea to mention Abuelita at all," I added. "She'd scare anyone off."

"Right. Good point. What kind of movies do you like?"

"Oh." I picked up my glass. "I'm a bit of a mixed bag. I like romcoms, but I also really like thrillers."

"Thrillers are fun. They're a favorite of mine, too. Do you have any hobbies?"

"Judging others and drinking wine." I tilted my glass from side to side to punctuate it. "You?"

"I watch a lot of sports."

"Oooh, that might be a dealbreaker. I'm not really into sports."

"I can make a deal not to watch it around you. I can cope with it."

"What happens if you need feeding on a Sunday?"

He grimaced. "Do you do a delivery service?"

"Do I look like Uber Eats?"

"No, you're very pretty."

I laughed and twirled some pasta onto my fork. "You'll just have to make sure you go and see your grandmother before a long day of watching sports."

"Ah, my totally not-crazy grandmother." He nodded. "That sounds like a good idea."

I smiled, putting the pasta into my mouth. Luke winked, sticking his fork into his lasagna.

I held his gaze for a second before dropping my eyes to the condensation on the table from our cold water glasses.

This wasn't so bad after all.

TWENTY

ASPEN

Thrillers and Thrills

"OKAY, NO, I DON'T BELIEVE YOU."

Luke laughed, nudging me with his elbow as we walked across the sand. "I swear. When she found out we were having dinner tonight, she sat down and told me all the excuses you'd told her about why you couldn't date any of my cousins, then asked me why I was so much better than all of them."

I shook my head and swung my shoes at my side. "I don't even remember why I turned them all down. I don't think I even gave her valid reasons half the time."

He shrugged, sticking his hands in his pockets. "She told me that I'm not allowed to fuck this up, because she's tried to marry you into this family for years, and this is the first promising sign that her plans are finally coming to fruition."

"She's insane. Now I know why y'all made a promise to each other to elope whenever you planned to get married."

"You know she's insane. It's not like it's a secret for you. The only question is whether or not you think you can deal with her if we started dating for real."

I snorted, stopping. "If we started dating? I think we've both come to the conclusion that, until this point, we've been dating without any kind of romantic feelings. It's not that much of a stretch, is it?"

"Does this mean we're finally over the whole 'best friend' thing being an issue?"

"No. Absolutely not." I shook my head. "It's going to be weird. You know that, right?"

Luke reached over and took my hand, then pulled me down to the sand with him. I set my shoes on the sand next to me and tucked my feet under my butt.

"I know it's gonna be weird," he said. "No matter how much we joke about it, we're still always going to have been best friends first. Adjusting from our normal relationship is going to be hard, but I don't want to lie, I want to try it."

"Do you think we can do it? Go from best friends to more?"

He nodded slowly, meeting my eyes and smiling. "I do. I think we'll need to work hard at it, but then again, tonight has been easy."

"Except for that bitch server who gave you her number." The audacity of the woman. We were clearly on a date, yet she'd had the balls to scrawl her number on the back of his receipt.

I'd wanted to go after her.

Luke had wrapped one arm around my waist and all but carried me out of the restaurant.

I was still a little annoyed about that.

"I know what you're thinking, and no, I do not regret hauling you out of the building." He kept his gaze focused on mine. "I've seen you get in a fight. It's not pretty."

I held up one finger. "I was nine, and Tammy Rosenthal had stolen my project and turned it in as her own. I'd spent two weeks on that damn solar system."

"Yes, and you slapped her like you were a seal trying to get someone's attention."

"Well, it worked, because she had to admit she'd stolen my solar system."

Luke rolled his eyes. "Still, I can't let anyone else witness that."

"Just as well. I'd have ripped her extensions right off her head."

"For giving me her number?"

"Did you or did you not have a hissy fit this week because some guy gave me his number? And we hadn't even agreed to go on a date?"

He opened his mouth, then stopped. "Totally different. I'm a guy. I was marking my territory."

"Okay, first, you're not a dog, and I'm not a tree trunk. Second, why can't I mark my territory?"

"Because you fight like a drunken seal."

"I should slap you for that."

"But you won't."

"You're a little too sure about that, don't you think?"

"Aspen, if you try to slap me, I'll grab your wrist and kiss you 'til you calm down."

I raised one eyebrow. "Try it, and I'll slap you even harder."

He grabbed me, pushing me to lie down on the sand. I laughed as I fell backward and he leaned over me. His blue eyes sparkled as he looked down, his gaze easily finding mine.

His body blocked out the setting sun, means shadows danced across his face, illuminating his strong features.

"What?" he asked, lips curving to one side.

"Nothing." I smiled back. "I'm just thinking it's weird that I've known for years how handsome you are, but the desire to sit on your face is totally new."

His lips twitched. "For what it's worth, you've always been hot, but the desire to have you sit on my face is also new."

"It's always nice to be on the same page." I grinned. "I thought you were kissing me."

"I was going to, but Mrs. Doncaster is walking her dog, and she's taking a 'pee break' by the tree up there. If I kiss you right now, the next thing she'll do is call all her friends at the bingo hall and tell them the guy who mooned them was kissing you."

"That is a valid reason to not kiss me." I laughed and pushed at him, making him sit up. "Why don't you take me home and kiss me there instead?"

"Are you inviting me in?"

"No. I told you, I'm not putting out on the first date."

"Fine." He sighed. "You'll regret that later tonight when you're having another dirty dream about me."

"I cannot possibly regret it as much as the first time." I got up and pulled my dress down, then grabbed my shoes.

"The first time? I don't know whether to ask you if that means there's been more or why the first one was the worst." Luke stood and brushed the sand off his hands. "Oh, God, the first one didn't reflect that night, did it?"

I shook my head with a laugh. "No, it didn't. Thank God. No offense, but I don't think I could relive that again."

"I'd be offended if I didn't feel the same." He unlocked his car and held open the passenger door for me. "So… The first time, huh?"

I got in and tugged the door shut until he'd joined me. "There may have been one more dirty dream, but I don't need to go into details."

"Yeah, you do. Were you sitting on my face?"

"I was sitting on the grave I'd just buried you in for asking me stupid questions."

He laughed and pulled away, turning toward my house. "Is the grave marked, at least?"

"No. You don't deserve a marker."

More laughter. "You're a delight. Why has Abuelita been so keen to marry you into my family, again?"

"I'm gonna say the number one reason is that she loves me."

"Yes, but why?"

"Same reason you love me."

"I love you because you feed me and didn't punch me for not giving you an orgasm the first time we had sex." He flashed me a grin.

"Mmm." I side-eyed him as we pulled into my apartment parking lot.

I didn't know why we couldn't walk. I literally lived minutes from downtown—which was right by the beach—because of work. But no, he wanted to be a gentleman and drive.

I slipped my feet back into my heels and winced as my toes crushed in the end.

Right. This was why we hadn't walked.

Heels.

Solid reason. My toes agreed.

Luke made it around to my door before I could grab the handle. He opened it, sweeping his arm for me to get out.

"I can open my own door, you know," I said, swinging my legs out of the car.

"On Earth, we say thank you."

I stood, gripping the top of the door. "Thank you."

"You're welcome." He smirked. "Also, have you met my grandmother? If she thought I was letting a lady open her own car door on a date, she'd bring out that damn flip-flop she's so fond of."

I shuddered and stepped up onto the sidewalk that ran the length of the parking lot. "I swear to God, just the mention of the shoe makes me never want to wear one again."

"Yep. Abuelita and her flip-flop will do that to a person." He locked the car and walked with me to the building door while I fumbled in my purse for my keys.

"So what you're telling me," I said, pulling out the keys, "Is that you're doing it less to be a gentleman, and more so Abuelita doesn't beat you with her shoe."

A tiny crease appeared on Luke's forehead. "Yep. Pretty much."

"Okay, this is why you're single."

"Were single."

"Have been single for a long time," I finally settled on.

He laughed, wrapping one arm around my shoulders and squeezing. "You do have a point. It'd take someone with questionable sanity to marry into my family."

"You're right. I mean, I have seen what it's done to your dad."

"Nah. He was like that anyway." He shrugged as we reached my apartment door. "But the insanity is a good skill to have around Abuelita."

"I've literally watched them argue over carrots."

"Yeah, well, this morning, they were arguing over Dad's drill. He's putting up some shelves in the office for Mom, and apparently, the drilling was interrupting Abuelita's daytime TV." He frowned. "She's recorded three entire seasons of Family Feud. I think she has a crush on Steve Harvey."

I tried not to laugh. I did. But the thought of her crushing on the hilarious host was just too much, and it burst out of me to the point I was laughing so hard I couldn't get my key in the door so I just slumped against it instead.

"All right, I know the idea is a little fucking stupid, but is it that funny?"

"Yes," I wheezed, standing up straight. "The idea that

Abuelita can love anything but cooking, marrying off her grandchildren, and torturing your dad is insane to me."

"Well, when you put it like that…" He shrugged as I finally slid the key in and unlocked the door.

I peered at him over my shoulder and stepped inside, still laughing. I put my purse on the table by the door, then stopped, looking up at him to meet his eyes. "I had fun tonight. Surprisingly."

"Surprisingly? Surely by now you know I'm a delight to be around." Luke's eyes twinkled teasingly.

"You know what I mean." I bit the inside of my cheek. "Thank you for tonight."

The glint of teasing left his eyes. "It was fun. So, do I get a second date?"

I dipped my head and laughed. "I think I can do that."

His lips curved until his smile reached his eyes. "Good," he murmured, leaning in. His hand cupped the back of my neck, and I flattened mine against his chest as his lips brushed over mine.

My heart skipped a beat.

It was just a small kiss. A soft one, a fleeting one, but it seemed to hold so much.

Luke stepped back, his thumb ghosting over the curve of my jaw. "Goodnight, Aspen."

I hugged the door, smiling as he left. "Night, Luke."

TWENTY-ONE

LUKE

Too Much Steve Harvey

"PENIS!" ABUELITA SCREAMED.

I froze, staring at Dad. "What the hell?"

"She's watching Family Feud again," he muttered, shooting a dark look in the direction of the living room. "Emmanuel was here last night and taught her how to use YouTube."

"Why would he do that?"

"To avoid her flip-flop."

Made sense. "What did he do this time?"

"Totaled his car. Again. After she bought him a new one."

I rolled my eyes and took the dish he handed me to put away. "She has to stop giving him money for cars. And he probably needs to learn how to drive again."

"It's his third car in two years. I don't think I've had three cars in thirty years."

"That's because you don't go anywhere, Dad."

"Not true. I go to hell and back every time your grandmother is awake."

Him and the rest of the family. "What's she watching on YouTube?"

"Cuts from the funniest bits of Family Feud. But I'm not sure she understood entirely what she was watching, so I've had a morning of her shouting inappropriate things at the TV."

I wrinkled my face up, right as she shouted, "Nipples!"

"Does she even know what she's yelling?" I asked.

Dad fixed me with a withering look. "I doubt it. I tried to ask, but she's taken to hiding her flip-flops around the house. She got a suspicious package from Amazon this week that I suspect is full of them."

"Is there no escaping it?"

"No, but I'm about to take up cleaning the house." He snorted. "Anyway, how did you date go last night?"

"My date?"

"With Aspen. Did you fuck it up?"

I took the bowls and put them in the cupboard. "No, I didn't fuck it up. It went well."

"Good." He nodded, grabbing the thing that held the cutlery and shoving it at me. "It's about time."

"What is?"

"The two of you getting together."

I paused, butter knife in hand, and peered at him out of the corner of my eye. "What does that mean?"

"I guess I always figured you would. You're different enough not to piss each other off but similar enough to get along. Plus, she puts up with the batshit crazy side of this family."

"Heard that," Mom said, sweeping through the kitchen and into the living room where she proceeded to talk to Abuelita in flawless Spanish.

I shook my head and turned to Dad. "You really thought we'd get together?"

"Honestly, I thought the two of you would have figured it out before now. You're such good friends and spend so much time together that either of you dating another person would be problematic."

Huh.

"Problematic?"

Dad sighed and took the sharp knives from the basket. "Yeah. Can you see any woman you'd date being comfortable with your close relationship with a beautiful woman?"

"No," I said slowly.

"And no man would ever be comfortable with his girlfriend spending so much time with you. Would you be?"

"No." I didn't need to think that through. "You're right. But that doesn't mean we should be together; it's just a sidenote."

"You're right. I think you should be together because you're clearly supposed to be."

"What?"

"Shit, it's like talking to a potato and expecting it to do algebra." Dad put the empty cutlery basket back in the dishwasher, then straightened and looked at me. "I always expected you to get together because you just make sense. You know each other inside out. You've seen each other through the best times of your lives and the absolute worst ones. When her grandfather died, you dropped everything to be there with her. She's there for every family wedding we've ever had. In fact, I think I'd disown you if you ever brought a girl home who isn't Aspen."

I laughed, resting my hands on the counter. "I'll keep that in mind, Dad, thanks."

"You're welcome." He grinned. "But, seriously, son— I don't have to be a genius to know that this will work out. One way or another."

"Are we talking about Aspen?" Mom walked in. "Hopefully, Mama will stop shouting genitals out now."

"That was quite the one-eighty." Dad pulled her into his side and kissed her hair. "Yes, we're talking about Aspen."

Mom's face lit up. "How was your date?"

I should have stayed at home. I knew better than to come here. Damn it.

"It went well," I said. "And yes, we're having a second date, and no, we aren't getting married yet."

"Yet. I'll take it." Mom winked and left the room. "Oh, honey?" She turned to Dad. "I found your drill. It was in the shower."

Dad's eyes widened. "Does it still work?"

Mom nodded. "She was just trying to scare you. I'm taking her to the doctor this afternoon, so you'll have two hours to finish those shelves up for me. If they don't get done then, I'm not responsible for what happens to it after that."

"Got it." Dad grimaced. "Where is the drill now?"

"In my panties drawer. She'll never look there." Mom shot him a sweet smile and disappeared.

Dad shook his head, sighed, and pinched the bridge of his nose. "Now, Luke, listen to me. You two might be meant for each other in my opinion, but remember this: when you marry someone, you don't just marry them. You marry their family."

"Aspen's family don't live here anymore."

"Oh, I know." He dropped his hand and met my eyes. "I was just making sure you know that means she'll get dragged into this shitshow."

I rubbed my mouth to hide my smile. "I think she'll be able to handle it."

"Puta!" Abuelita shouted at the TV. "Is a puta!"

We both jerked our heads in her direction.

"What kind of questions are they asking where 'whore' is a correct answer?" I asked.

Dad shrugged. "Told you. Shitshow."

"JUSTIN, IF YOU HIT ON ME ONE MORE TIME, I'm going to grab a lemon from the bowl behind me, bend you over like a little bitch in prison, and shove it up your ass." Aspen slammed her hand down on the top of the bar. "Are we clear?"

Justin reached over and grabbed her hand. "No ring. You're fair game, honey."

He was doing it just to piss her off now.

"Honey? I'm gonna honey your ass!"

"Please do." He grinned.

Tom nudged me with his elbow. "You just gonna let him piss her off like that?"

I nodded, drinking from my beer.

Aspen turned fiery eyes on me. "Aren't you supposed to be a gentleman? Do you hear this jerk?"

I put down my bottle and held out my hands. "Whoa. Two days ago, you were adamant you could open your own door. I thought this fell into that category."

"Yeah, opening a car door and one of your friends being a total tool is exactly the same."

Blaire came back from the bathroom and whacked Justin around the back of his head with a sharp slap. "Back the fuck off." She walked back to her seat between me and Tom, then did the same to me. "Grow a pair, Luke."

"Fucking hell. Is your hand made of concrete?" I rubbed the back of my head.

Blaire smiled dreamily at me then turned to Aspen. "I got your back. I'll be your boyfriend if he won't. I probably hit harder."

Tom smirked at me.

"Yeah, but you don't have a dick," I reminded her.

"Judging by your silence, I've got bigger balls."

"Remind me why you like her." I looked at Tom.

He grinned.

"Because," Blaire said, "I'm an oral magician."

Aspen grimaced. "That's too much information for a Sunday night."

"I like how nobody commented on the boyfriend thing," Tom interjected. "Does that mean it's official?"

"No, it means nobody pays any attention to Blaire's crap," Aspen replied. "You're no rookie, Tom. You know that."

He nodded, earning himself a glare from his girlfriend.

I laughed, keeping my eyes on Aspen. While it was no secret now that we were seeing each other—thanks mostly to the local bingo club and the post office—we hadn't discussed labels.

Just that we were dating.

And after what my dad said yesterday, we didn't need to label anything. The more I'd thought about what he'd said, the more I realized he was right.

We did make sense. There didn't have to be a reason for it. We just did.

We knew everything there was to know about each other, and while we'd initially used that as a reason not to act on our newfound feelings, I was beginning to think otherwise.

We didn't have to tread carefully, trying to figure out where we stood with one another. There would be no awkward family meets. No trying to work out how to handle an argument with each other—what was the other person's temper like? Did they hold a grudge? How soon was it to call again?

We knew all those things. Just like how I knew about her hatred of certain hair ties, she probably knew all the little things about me that I paid no attention to.

We didn't just know each other.

We knew each other. The way couples who've been married for thirty years know each other. We knew the ins and outs and ups and downs of our relationship.

I knew that when she was mad at me, I had to leave her for a minimum of twelve hours until she'd been able to eat, nap, and take a shower.

The three things she always did when she was angry.

And I knew I didn't get mad at her. Not the way she got mad, anyway.

Then again, I didn't think anyone got mad the way Aspen got mad, so Justin was really pushing his luck tonight.

She glanced over at me, finally meeting my eyes, and a small smile tugged at her lips before she looked away almost shyly.

What we had was the perfect basis to build a relationship on.

All we needed to do was figure out how to fall in love, and given that two minutes of bad, drunken sex had kickstarted other feelings inside us, I didn't think that would be too hard.

I'd never thought about falling in love with her until now. It'd never been a blip on my radar until now, and now, it was blaring at me. Falling in love with Aspen Camden would be so easy. Like flicking a light switch.

After all, I didn't need to uncover all the things I'd love

about her.

I already knew them, and I already loved them.

"So, what's on the cards for tonight's second date?" Blaire asked, looking between me and Aspen.

"She got to pick this one," I replied.

"Ah. So you're watching a movie in yoga pants."

"Nailed it," Aspen called from the other end of the bar.

"I'm not wearing yoga pants." I twisted my bottle. "Not in a million years."

Blaire smiled slyly. "I bet you won't be wearing any pants by the end of it."

Tom choked on a laugh, and I just about did the same, 'cause hey. I wouldn't complain if that was how it ended.

"Pants will be staying firmly on," Aspen added, rejoining us. "No putting out until the third date."

"Doesn't count." Blaire shook her head. "The third date rule only applies if you didn't put out already. And since you did that…"

"Told you," I muttered.

"Carry on." Aspen met my eyes, her face expressionless. "And the only thing putting out is gonna be your right hand."

"Yeah, I'll be putting it across your backside."

Blaire grinned. "This is fun. I didn't think I'd like you two dating, but I take it back. You're kind of frisky."

"What's wrong with us dating?" Aspen said. "You're

the one who shoved me into it!"

"Nice to know you did it of your own accord." I snorted.

"Shh." She held up a finger and focused on Blaire. "What the hell?"

Blaire held up her hands. "You're both my best friends. Whose side do I take in a fight? Is it automatic? Does my opinion matter?"

"Mine!" Aspen stared at her, open-mouthed. "You always take my side."

"What did I do?" I asked. "What if it's your fault?"

"Doesn't matter. I'm gonna win anyway."

"See?" Blaire interjected, waving her hands. "You're my best friend, but Luke has Abuelita and her tacos."

It was nice to know my friends were only here for my grandmother's cooking.

"I have her tacos," Aspen replied. "I practically have her home restaurant in my kitchen."

"That is a good point," Blaire mused. "But if y'all break up, you don't have Abuelita's anything."

I sighed. "Sadly, Abuelita will probably assume it's all my fault, beat me with her flip-flop, and move Aspen in so she can heal her broken heart with tacos and salsa."

"I'd be okay with that, for the record," Aspen added. "Actually, Blaire, you take Luke's side. I'll have Abuelita on mine."

"Yeah, that's what you want," Tom said, barely able to contain his laughter. "A five-foot-tall, crazy Mexican woman with way too many flip-flops and a bit of a temper. That's how you win arguments."

Actually, it was. At least in my family.

Aspen looked at me. "Clearly, he's not familiar with la chancla."

"The world would be a better place if nobody was. Including Abuelita." I snorted.

Blaire nodded, wincing. "That thing hurts. Remember that night we camped in your backyard and snuck out to a party? She waited in the tent for us to come back and beat us all."

"That was the first and only time I ever snuck out." I shook my head.

"Same," Aspen added. "I was so afraid that she'd just know, even though I grew up on the opposite side of town. I had nightmares for a month after that night."

"I still have them!" Blaire shuddered. "I don't think I've worn flip-flops since."

"Speak for yourself," Aspen said. "Sandals or nothing for me." She checked the time on her phone under the bar. "Oh, I'm done." She looked at me with a smile. "Let me go get Dec, and we can go, okay?"

"Sure." I nodded while she disappeared to the back.

Blaire nudged me. "You're really doing it. I'm a little

surprised."

"We all are," Justin drawled from a few feet away, sipping on his beer.

"You want another slap?" Blaire snapped.

Man. He really was like the chalk to their cheese.

"Yes, we're doing it," I said to her, ignoring Justin. "Or we're trying to. It might all go down in flames yet."

"Well, as long as Aspen doesn't have the match, you'll be just fine. With her hidden temper, she'd burn the whole town down."

Tom frowned. "Aspen has a hidden temper?"

Blaire and I nodded.

"It takes a lot to get her there, but when she does…" I blew out a breath.

Blaire, however, smirked. "It's why she'll fit in perfectly in Luke's family. They've all got tempers."

I wanted to deny it.

Couldn't.

My family was a shit show.

"Ready?" Aspen came bouncing out of the staff door, her phone in one hand and her purse in the other.

"Ready." I finished my beer and stood up. "Although I should warn you, I forgot to bring my sweatpants."

She sighed and met my eyes with a knowing glint in hers. "Of course you did."

TWENTY-TWO

ASPEN

Trick or Treat… Or Both?

"I KNEW YOU DIDN'T FORGET THEM deliberately," I muttered into Luke's shoulder. My heart was still racing because, yes, I put out.

And I didn't even wait until the end of the date.

In my defense, it wasn't my fault that my yoga pants turned him on. It was all his fault, really, for forgetting his sweats. I didn't have any of his stuff here, so it wasn't even as if I could pull a pair out of one of my drawers.

And, no, if you were wondering, the sex last time was not a fluke.

"I swear, it was an accident," he murmured, trailing his fingertip in little circles on my shoulder. "A happy one."

"Full of shit." I moved and pushed up so I could prop my head on my hand and look down at him. "It was a deliberate move, and you know it."

"Can you blame me? It's not like sweatpants could hide my erection anyway. I'd turn them into a tent."

"I get it. You have a big, magic cock. You don't need to keep trying to convince me you're good in bed anymore." I patted his chest and sat up, swinging my legs to the side.

I'd moved too fast. The blood rushed to my head, and I set my hand out to steady myself while I blinked the pressure away.

"Yeah, you're right, I don't." He laughed and got up, leaving the room with his cock in his hand.

Damn it. He was going to beat me to the bathroom.

I pushed up and ran after him. I knew I couldn't beat him, but it was all right for him. Gravity worked in his favor after sex.

It did not work in mine.

Grabbing a wad of tissue, I stuck it between my legs.

"That's hot," Luke said, turning on my shower.

"Why can't I shower first?"

"You wanna share?"

"Are you normally like this on second dates?"

"No, but we've already established we're not a normal couple. So, you wanna share?"

"No, I want to go first. Gravity is not my friend right now!"

He looked at the tissue between my legs and smirked.

"That's the sign of good sex."

"It's the sign I'm about to rip the showerhead off the wall and beat you with it."

Luke laughed, stepping aside for me.

"Thank you." I jumped under the water and screamed.

It was ice-cold, and it was beating down on me like torrential rain.

I stepped immediately out of the shower and almost slipped, the small rug on the floor being the only thing saving me from an almost certain trip to the emergency room.

Luke was laughing. Hard.

"This relationship isn't starting well, Luke."

"Oh, it's a relationship now, is it?"

"It's about to be your death," I shot back. "I hate you."

"Nah, you don't."

"Try me."

"It's impossible to hate anyone who can make you orgasm as hard as I just did."

I sighed and turned the dial so hot water came through instead. Making sure to test the water before I got in, I stuck my hand under the stream and waiting for it to get just right.

It only took me a couple of minutes to rinse off my body. I left the water running for Luke while I dried off and wrapped my robe around me. All I needed was some panties, and I'd be set.

To finish the movie we interrupted.

I didn't even know what we'd been watching.

Leaving him in the shower singing 'Sex Bomb' to himself, I went back to my room for my panties. I'd just pulled them up over my knees when there was a knock at my door.

I tugged my underwear up properly and walked toward the door. "Who is it?"

"Is me!"

Oh no.

Oh no, no, no, no.

"Uh, just a sec!" I darted back to the bathroom, panic racing through me. "It's Abuelita! She's at the door!"

Luke jerked around so fast he almost slipped himself. "What? What the fuck is she doing here?"

I shook my head quickly. I didn't know. I couldn't just ask her through the door, could I?

He quickly got out of the shower, soap still on the side of his neck, and wrapped a towel around his waist. "Go answer it!"

"Like this?" I hissed. "She'll know what we've been doing!"

"Asp, she's been yelling genital and cuss words at Steve Harvey for three days."

"What?"

"Long story. Just answer the door before she starts

yelling genitals at us!"

This was it. This was where my life ended. This was the beginning of the end.

I was going to die of embarrassment.

At least I was wearing panties.

I took a deep breath while Luke chickened out and ran into the bedroom. Oh, God.

I unlocked the front door and smiled. "Abuelita. What a nice surprise."

She lifted up a brown paper bag, and the smell of food hit me in the face, making my stomach rumble. "I bring food for date!"

"Oh. We were going to order some—"

"Nonsense. I cook. I bring. You eat." She pushed her way past me and took herself into my kitchen.

Excellent.

This couldn't get worse.

Luke walked out of my room wearing his jeans and not his t-shirt. "Abuelita! What are you doing here?"

"I bring food," she said, looking over at him.

She froze.

Her eyes ran up and down his half-naked body, then she turned her head so she could look at me.

In my llama robe.

With my messy hair.

A slow, knowing smile spread across her face. "Ah, you

need food."

Oh, hell.

My cheeks burned.

"You busy, sí?" She waggled her eyebrows.

I stared at Luke.

"Abuelita, we appreciate the food, but we are having a date." He gently took her by the shoulders and spun her around.

"Sí. You make me baby, yes?"

I inhaled sharply, my eyes going wide, and I spun around with my hands out. "No, no, no baby."

"Oh. You should make me baby." She broke out of Luke's hold in the doorway and turned to him, touching his cheek. She reeled off a couple of sentences in Spanish, ones that made Luke's jaw twitch before she came to me.

She clasped my face and kissed me on each cheek before she left.

Luke waited until she was out of earshot, then slammed the door shut.

"What did—what did she just say?"

"She told me she spoke to the guy who runs her church. He has the third Sunday in September free if we'd like a fall wedding."

I blinked. "What? Is she crazy?"

"Yes," he said slowly. "We've known that for a long time."

"Did she book it?"

"It's on hold."

"Have you considered taking her to a psychiatrist?"

"Yes." He nodded. "Mom got la chancla last time it was brought up."

I shuddered and went to the bag of food. "Isn't she a Catholic?"

"Yes."

"Don't you have to be Catholic to get married in a Catholic church?"

He shrugged and pulled out the containers. They were full of steaming, hot food, including homemade chips and dips. "I don't know. I haven't been since I was twelve."

"Well, I'm not a Catholic, so there goes that plan."

"She'll try to convert you."

"We're eloping to Vegas. And not on the third Saturday in September." I met his eyes over the island, and we both burst out laughing.

It was so ridiculous. Yes, the woman was insane, and yes, we knew that, but this was next-level craziness.

Yet, it felt strangely perfect. It didn't freak me out, because I knew Abuelita, and I knew she was simply passionate about her family. All she wanted was for them to be happy, even if she showed it in weird little ways.

Like showing up after sex with food and holding a wedding date in a church… After two dates.

Not that the dates counted the same for us.

We didn't have to date the way most people did. We didn't need to get to know each other, because we'd already done that.

All we needed to learn to do was let go of our self-imposed boundaries and just let the cards fall where they may.

But there would be no September wedding.

At least not this year.

Besides, I always imagined getting married in the Spring. Which, in Texas, is around the new year.

I laughed, dropping my head down.

"What?"

"It's crazy," I said, meeting his eyes. "Don't you think? Literally, any other girl would have run out of that door by now if they'd just had that conversation with your grandmother, yet here I am, opening a Tupperware tub with homemade nachos in, thinking it's entirely normal."

His laugh was deep—a proper belly laugh that sent tingles across my skin.

Luke walked around the kitchen island and wrapped his arms around my shoulders, drawing me into his body. Both of us were shaking with now-quiet laughter, and I wound my arms around his waist.

"It is, sadly, normal," he chuckled into my hair. "Which is why we make total sense together, Asp. You get it."

"I've been around long enough." One last laugh escaped my lips, and I leaned back to look up into his eyes. "You really think we make sense?"

His smile was lopsided, but there was a warmth in his eyes that made my heart skip. "Yeah. I think we make perfect sense."

"You think we can actually do this?"

"I know we can." He leaned his head down and brushed his nose against mine. "As long as you can put up with Abuelita."

"Well, I've done it for twenty years already. At least she won't be setting me up with your cousins anymore."

He laughed, tilting his head so his lips brushed over mine. "There is always that. Now, she'll just be marrying you off to me instead."

"I can cope with that," I whispered against his lips.

"Good." He kissed me once, twice, three times. "Can I tell you something?"

"Sure."

"I think you'd be pretty easy to fall in love with, Aspen Camden."

I blushed, smiling. "Can I tell you something?"

"Sure."

"Our food is getting cold."

He slapped my ass as I darted away, laughing. I snatched a chip from one of the tubs, grinning as I bit down into it.

"Here I thought you were going to say something nice to me back," Luke grumbled, opening the tub with burritos in.

"I could fall in love with you," I said, tilting my head to the side. "Maybe on the third Sunday in September."

He laughed, peering at me through thick eyelashes, and threw a Tupperware lid at me. "I want that in writing."

I crunched on another chip, still grinning.

Yeah.

We were going to be just fine.

EPILOGUE
ASPEN

Tequila Forever

EIGHTEEN MONTHS LATER

"TEQUILA IS THE PERFECT NAME FOR A DOG!"

"Yes, but we're not talking about getting a dog. We're talking about getting a cat." Luke flattened his palms on the island. "And Tequila is a dreadful name. I've already told you that about five hundred times."

I pressed my hand to my chest and gasped. "How could you say that? You'd still be single and eating my food if it weren't for tequila!"

"Yes, and now I live in your apartment, give you regular orgasms, and I still eat your food."

"Exactly. You have tequila to thank. You can pay homage to it and years of hangovers by calling our dog Tequila."

"We aren't getting a dog. And I'm not paying homage to a drunken tap-tap-squirt." His lips twitched. "We're getting a cat."

"I don't like cats."

"I don't like dogs."

"Lies. You like Blaire."

He bent forward, burying his face in his hands. "I can't do this. Why don't we get a hamster instead?"

I groaned and dropped onto the sofa, looking across the apartment at him. "Because they smell and don't care if you've been gone all day. I want to come home and know I've been missed when I've been at work."

"Hey, I miss you when you're at work."

"Luke, when I got in last night, you grabbed my ass and asked me if I minded you finishing your video game before we went to bed."

He threw his arms out to the side. "I grabbed your ass! That's affectionate. I missed you."

"No, you grabbed my ass because you wanted to finish your video game, then go and have sex."

"But that's what happened."

"Still not a dog."

He sighed and walked over to me. "We're gonna have to flip a coin for it."

"I'm not flipping a coin on a pet," I said hotly. "It's a dog, or it's nothing. And I want one of those beagles from

Gerald at the horse ranch."

"You and those fucking beagles." He rolled his eyes. "We're gonna have to think on it until we can compromise."

"Fine." I sighed and propped my elbow on the back of the sofa so I could rest my head on my hand. "We'll put it to bed to just come back to it next week."

"There's my girl." He kissed the top of my head. "By the way, a package arrived for you today. Were you expecting something?"

I sat up. "Ooh, my new hairdryer!"

"Exciting," he muttered. "It's in the bedroom. I'll get it."

I bounced on the sofa until he returned with the box. "That's a big box for a hairdryer."

"I told you to stop shopping online. It's five percent your order, ninety-five percent packaging."

"Yes, but online shopping means I don't have to speak to people. Why is the box open?"

He shrugged, putting his hands in his pockets. "I wanted to see what it was, but I couldn't get past the packaging, so I gave up."

I rolled my eyes and scooted to the edge of the cushion. The box moved.

"The box moved." I looked at Luke. "Why did it move?"

His lips twitched.

Eyeing him, I reached to open the box and looked inside.

And squealed.

"What did you do?" I breathed, reaching in and pulling out the tiny beagle puppy. "Oh, hello, beautiful."

"Meet Tequila," he said dryly. "I was thinking Patches, but whatever."

I held the tiny puppy close to my chest, looking at him in wonder. "But what? How? You just told me you hate dogs!"

"Yeah, well, Gerald needed some work doing on one of his barns two weeks ago. I went out there to see him, and he let me take a look at the puppies. She wouldn't leave me alone and cried when I left, so I pretty much handed him the money there and then." He raised his shoulders and dropped them again. "What can I say? She won me over."

"Oh. You are my favorite." I held the puppy at arm's length to look at her.

"Me or Tequila?"

"I haven't decided yet." She was so cute. So tiny. Like you could put her in your purse tiny. "And you got her a collar!"

It was pink. Leather.

And…glinting.

I froze as my eyes zeroed in on the glint. "Luke," I said. "What did you do?" Slowly, I turned my head, and he was on the floor.

On one knee.

In front of me.

I brought the puppy down to my lap before I dropped her. My hands were shaking as he leaned forward and took off her collar. He fiddled with it for a second and pulled the ring off.

I stared at him.

Oh, my God.

"I figured she'd break the ice." His lips pulled to one side. "And potentially work in my favor."

I pressed my hand to my mouth.

"I mean, our relationship started with tequila, so I figured it fitted that we start the next part with Tequila."

Oh, my God.

"Aspen, will you marry me?"

I could do nothing but nod my head frantically. Partly because I was holding a puppy, and partly because the lump in my throat would choke me if I tried to speak. So I kept nodding, over and over, until he became nothing but a blur in front of me.

He sat on the sofa and pulled me in close to him. "Mom said the puppy and the ring would be too much. I should have listened."

I laughed, pressing my face into his shoulder. He took the squirming puppy from me so I could throw my arms around his neck. I had chills—all the good kinds.

"How long have you planned this?" I whispered through my tears.

"Well, I've had the ring for about six months."

"Six months?" I jerked back, wiping my eyes. "What?"

"I was trying to figure out how to ask you. Then she happened." He held up Tequila who was trying frantically to lick his face. "And I knew."

He tucked her against his body and picked the ring up from the table with the other hand. Gently, he pushed the ring down my finger, then smiled at me. "Who knew a tap-tap-squirt would end this well?"

I laughed, both of us falling back on the sofa. Tequila finally broke free of Luke's grasp and launched herself at his face, pretty much smothering him in puppy belly. He coughed and sputtered beneath her, and I fell back laughing, holding my stomach.

"Stop it. Damn it, Tequila. Pah—I have dog hair in my mouth!" Luke sputtered.

I laughed even harder, reaching and removing the tiny creature from his head.

"This is why I wanted a cat," he said, pointing at me, then sticking out his tongue to remove a hair.

I grinned, lifting my chin so Tequila could lick my neck.

Luke stalked into the kitchen to get water. He washed his mouth out once and looked over at me, trying to frown, but he couldn't. He smiled, eyes bright and happy, and I couldn't help but grin back as Tequila took my shoulders for a climbing frame.

It was a universally accepted truth that sleeping with your best friend was a very, very bad idea.

But spending forever with him?

Now that was a damn good idea.

THE END

Thank you so much for reading Tequila Tequila!

If you're interested in reading more from me, read on for the blurb from my upcoming romantic comedy,
CATASTROPHE QUEEN!

CATASTROPHE QUEEN

One hot mess. One hot boss. One too many hot encounters.

It's not you. It's me.

No, seriously. It is me. Not only does my name literally mean "unfortunate," but that's the story of my life.

Everything I touch turns to crap. An apartment fire—that I swear I was not responsible for—means I'm living back at home with my sex-mad parents. *Yay, me!*

Which is why I need my new job as personal assistant to Cameron Reid to get back on my feet. Three months in this job and I can move back out and, hopefully, remember to turn off my flat iron once in a while.

Ahem.

On paper, my job is easy. Make coffee. Book appointments. Keep everything in order.

Until I walk in on my boss, half-naked, wearing nothing but the kind of tiny white towel that dreams are made of.

Now, nothing is easy—except our mutual attraction. But he's my boss, and you know what they say about mixing work and pleasure: unless you do porn, it's just not worth it.

Or is it?

PRE-ORDER:
www.emmahart.org/catastrophe-queen

BOOKS BY EMMA HART

Standalones:

Blind Date

Being Brooke

Catching Carly

Casanova

Mixed Up

Miss Fix-It

Miss Mechanic

The Upside to Being Single

The Hook-Up Experiment

The Dating Experiment

Four Day Fling

Best Served Cold

Tequila Tequila

The Vegas Nights series:

Sin

Lust

Stripped series:

Stripped Bare

Stripped Down

The Burke Brothers:
Dirty Secret
Dirty Past
Dirty Lies
Dirty Tricks
Dirty Little Rendezvous

The Holly Woods Files:
Twisted Bond
Tangled Bond
Tethered Bond
Tied Bond
Twirled Bond
Burning Bond
Twined Bond

By His Game series:
Blindsided
Sidelined
Intercepted

Call series:
Late Call
Final Call
His Call

Wild series:

Wild Attraction

Wild Temptation

Wild Addiction

Wild: The Complete Series

The Game series:

The Love Game

Playing for Keeps

The Right Moves

Worth the Risk

Memories series:

Never Forget

Always Remember

ABOUT THE AUTHOR

Emma Hart is the New York Times and USA TODAY bestselling author of over thirty novels and has been translated into several different languages.

She is a mother, wife, lover of wine, Pink Goddess, and valiant rescuer of wild baby hedgehogs.

Emma prides herself on her realistic, snarky smut, with comebacks that would make a PMS-ing teenage girl proud.

Yes, really. She's that sarcastic.

You can find her online at:
www.emmahart.org
www.facebook.com/emmahartbooks
www.instagram.com/EmmaHartAuthor
www.pinterest.com/authoremmahart

Alternatively, you can join her reader group at http://bit.ly/EmmaHartsHartbreakers.

You can also get all things Emma to your email inbox by signing up for Emma Alerts*. http://bit.ly/EmmaAlerts

*Emails sent for sales, new releases, pre-order availability, and cover reveals. Each cover reveal contains an exclusive excerpt.